JUNIOR YEAR ABROAD

By Howard R. Simpson

JUNIOR YEAR ABROAD

HOWARD R. SIMPSON

PUBLISHED FOR THE CRIME CLUB BY
DOUBLEDAY & COMPANY, INC.
GARDEN CITY, NEW YORK
1986

All the characters in this book
are fictitious, and any resemblance
to actual persons, living or dead,
is purely coincidental.

Library of Congress Cataloging-in-Publication Data
Simpson, Howard R., 1925–
Junior year abroad.
I. Title.
PS3569.I49J83 1986   813'.54   85-13184
ISBN 0-385-23260-8

First Edition

To Shawn and Malek

JUNIOR YEAR ABROAD

CHAPTER I

It was the coldest November in twenty-eight years. A biting wind slashed through the streets of Aix-en-Provence, pummeled the glass-enclosed café terraces and rattled the shutters of the old, thick-walled buildings off the Cours Mirabeau. Frost halos formed around the streetlights, and cabdrivers gathered in the bars near the Place Général de Gaulle to drink coffee and rum while their cabs sat unused at their stands.

The streets were surprisingly empty for a university town. Those students who weren't still in class were seeking warmth in their Spartan dormitories or rented rooms. The more adventurous had braved the cold weather, rushing red-nosed and swathed in woolens to their favorite cafés for hot chocolate or *vin chaud*. Patches of snow from a brief morning fall clung to the tile roofs. Gray pigeons sheltered motionless beside the smoking chimney pots like misplaced displays from a taxidermist's window.

A portable gas heater hissed in a corner of a small studio apartment off the Place des Tanneurs. A fat, rust-colored cat lay on a foldaway bed, licking its paws. The clatter and bang of firewood being unloaded in the nearby alley was muffled by the closed shutters. Someone was singing out in the street. The voice was high and clear, but it faded and died as the singer moved on.

The nude girl lay face down half in and half out of the bathroom shower, her black hair a damp, bloody mop, clogging the drain. She had fallen with one leg over the other. Her right arm was braced elbow up, as if she had tried to raise herself. Her flesh was mottled purple and pink. A series of raw, swollen puncture wounds covered her upper back and neck. The indented channels leading to the shower drain were dark with coagulating blood.

The cat stirred, stretching. It jumped from the bed and walked slowly to the bathroom door. It paused a moment, sniffing. Then it moved cautiously to the body and began licking the dead girl's toe.

The three-story eighteenth-century town house on the rue Aude occupied by Willington University's Foreign Studies Program was brightly lit. A reception honoring Madame Emmanuelle de Rozier, dean of foreign students at the University of Aix-en-Provence, was in progress. It was an annual ritual, with the announced purpose of bringing Willington's newly arrived junior-year-abroad students into informal contact with Madame de Rozier and her faculty. The real purpose of the event was the need to pay homage to Madame de Rozier's position in the local academic community. Several American universities maintained study programs in Aix. Most of them worked in direct collaboration with Madame de Rozier's faculty. All vied for her favor. The year's study of French language, history and culture offered by the American institutions would have been impossible without her cooperation and blessing.

The Willington program was a comparative newcomer to Aix, and Dr. Ronald Gregg, the director, had made a special effort to ensure an impressive social effort. One of the best caterers in town had been hired. Madame de Rozier's favorite champagne was on hand, and she had been asked to preview and comment on the final invitation list.

Standing in the reception area waiting to greet his guests, Dr. Gregg reflected on the strange mix of French and American academia flowing through the rooms of the Willington house. Chubby French professors in dark, three-piece suits, stuffing themselves with canapés of smoked salmon and lumpfish caviar, contrasted sharply with his disheveled students, in shapeless jackets and winter boots. He noted with disapproval that the Willington students, concentrating on the drinks, had become louder as the party progressed. His faculty members were identifiable by their tweedy, eastern-seaboard look. Too old to be students, almost too young to be professors, they grasped at their own fading youth with desperation, wanting both respect and friendship from their students. Dr. Gregg had long since passed that stage. He was tall and thin. A thatch of shortly cropped silver hair accentuated his tanned, sharp face. The dark tortoiseshell frames of his spectacles gave him a scholarly air, befitting his position.

A blast of cold air from the doorway signaled more guests. A professor and his wife from the Luminy campus, near Marseille, were being helped out of their coats as Gregg went forward to greet them. A tray of champagne glasses appeared, and Gregg served the new arrivals before passing them on to one of his assistants. Momentarily alone, he scanned the nearby music room looking for Madame de Rozier. She was in a far corner—the pivot of a galaxy of revolving sycophants.

Bone thin in a black organdy gown of many tucks and flourishes, Madame de Rozier was standing by the piano, her champagne glass held delicately at shoulder height, listening to a bearded Willington student. The youth towered over her and was leaning forward to make himself heard in the din of conversation. Rumor had it that Madame de Rozier had just reached sixty-eight, but it was hard to tell from her appearance. Her dyed hair rose in a black puff over a face crusted with powder. That woman, Gregg mused, could be sixty or eighty . . . or more.

"It's going well." Marcia Chappel, Gregg's administrative assistant, was by his side. "We have a full house."

"As the French would say," he replied, "all Aix is here."

"Can I get you a drink?" Miss Chappel asked.

"I'll wait for the *sous-préfet*'s arrival. Don't want to greet him with a glass in my hand."

"Well, I'm off for a refill."

He watched Marcia move off through the crowd. She was not an unattractive woman. She hid a good figure under conservative suits and high-collared blouses. There were times he'd caught himself watching her in the office, times when a certain stance revealed the lines and curves of her body. But he shunted such thoughts aside. His world of academic achievement and success allowed no margin for sexual risk. Besides, she drank too much.

The arrival rate had slackened. The sous-préfet was late, but Gregg decided he could leave the door. It was time to devote some attention to Madame de Rozier. He moved toward the piano, smiling and nodding to his guests.

"Chère Madame," he said, approaching the guest of honor. "Are you being looked after?"

Madame de Rozier turned toward him with a tight scarlet smile.

"My dear Dr. Gregg. I am having a delightful time." She waved her empty champagne glass toward the bearded student. "Monsieur . . . ah?"

"Stevens," the student prompted.

"Yes, of course. Monsieur Stevens was telling me about Arizona . . . the land of sunshine."

"Good," Gregg said. "Please have some more champagne."

Stevens took the empty glass. "I'll be right back," he said.

Madame de Rozier moved closer to Gregg. "A charming boy. You always have such interesting students."

"We try to get the best."

"Tell me, are you pleased with this year's group?"

"Yes, we are. They all seem serious. The first round of exams will tell the story."

Madame de Rozier flashed a humorless smile. Her large, dark eyes swept over the other guests.

"May I offer some advice?" she asked.

"Certainly."

"Some American universities have had trouble in the past," she told Gregg. "Not enough control, a certain lack of discipline. It is very important to build a good reputation if your institution is to operate here with success."

"I agree," Gregg replied, wondering if he was getting her message correctly. "We are determined to establish a high academic standard for our students."

"Yes, that is most important. But you must realize that ours is a very old and conservative environment. Some of your American colleagues tend to forget that, and their work has been ruined."

Gregg was puzzled. "I don't quite—"

"Oh, it is simple enough. Grades and academic standards are one thing. But reputation and standing are just as important. You are outsiders here. Welcome, of course, but outsiders nonetheless. It will take a few years before you find full acceptance for the Willington program. During that time there must be no scandals. Do you understand?"

Gregg began to smile, but he saw that Madame de Rozier was quite serious.

"Madame," he responded gravely, "I assure you, there will be no scandals."

Again the brief slash of a smile and a quick nod. *"Cher monsieur,* I am pleased we understand each other."

The bearded student reappeared with Madame de Rozier's champagne and handed the glass to her with a flourish. Marcia Chappel waved to Gregg from across the room and pointed to the door. The sous-préfet and his wife had just arrived.

"If you'll excuse me," Gregg said, "the sous-préfet is here."

"But of course, do take care of your guests," Madame de Rozier told him. "I am in good hands."

A group of students were clustered around a serving table laden with trays of hors d'oeuvres, small sandwiches and a circular board filled with cheeses and buttered slices of coarse country bread.

"Delicious!" Hank Castel commented, his mouth full. "This goat's cheese is terrific."

"That sounds awful," Jean Bates commented, munching on an olive and frowning at the spread of food. "No dips, no chips, not even popcorn." She was a young blonde with an opulent figure, a blouse much too tight for her and contact lenses that were constantly shifting.

"What are those?" she asked, pursing her lips and squinting at the hors d'oeuvres.

"Mussels . . . *moules.* They're very tasty." Castel lifted one on a toothpick and popped it into his mouth.

"They look gross."

Castel took a sip of champagne. He'd only known Jean Bates for a few weeks, but he'd quickly lost interest in her. She was the perennial pom-pom girl, very much out of her element in a European setting. Why she'd come to Aix he'd never know. She was already homesick and spent most of her time at "Le Quick," a French version of McDonald's, where she could feed her frustrations with burgers and French fries. Castel had already classed her as an airhead.

"See you," he said, drifting off, leaving her to talk with another male student. He moved to a corner where he could watch the guests. Hank Castel was dark-haired and athletic, with the shoulders of a linebacker. Seeing him for the first time, most people would expect him to be an all-American jock. They were wrong. Castel was a straight-A student with a deep interest in European history and a determination to make the most of his year in France. His mother and father were first-generation Americans. Their families had come from the French Pyrénées. His visit to France was a form of homecoming.

Castel surveyed the ornate room with subdued excitement. The high, exquisitely painted plaster ceilings, the heavy scarlet drapes, the gold-framed mirrors reflecting the candlelight from the tables, the ancient parquet floors and the large, pink-marble fireplace formed an *ambiance* he'd imagined while studying French history and language during his freshman and sophomore years. He watched Dr. Gregg leading the sous-préfet and his wife through a series of introductions on the far side of the room. He imagined them as actors in an eighteenth-century play. Only the costumes have changed, he told himself.

"Hank"—Jean Bates was tugging at his arm—"I'm worried about Ginnie. She should be here by now."

"What?" he asked, jolted from his reverie.

"Ginnie. She went back to the studio to change and she hasn't shown up. It's not like her."

"She can take care of herself," he replied, wishing Jean Bates would find someone else to confide in. He glanced at the door. It was true, Ginnie was not there. He wished she were. Ginnie Feldman was both attractive and intelligent. It was a shame the housing office had given her Jean Bates as a roommate.

"Well," Jean Bates declared, "I'm going after her. You coming?"

"Oh, for God's sake!"

"Never mind. I'll go alone."

Hank Castel put his champagne glass down on a nearby table and caught up with Jean Bates as she hurried toward the door.

"All right," he said, grabbing her arm, "let's get it over with."

The Corvette bar, on the Quai des Belges, was warm and crowded. Marseille was under a cold drizzle. The neon lights of the Vieux Port shimmered in the dampness. Inspector Roger Bastide, seated at a small table, sipped a cloudy *pastis* while he read a story in *Le Figaro* about the Minister of the Interior's plans to fight terrorism. The writer had interviewed police officials in Paris and come away convinced that the police were not happy with the expanded role the Gendarmerie National was to play in the counterterrorist effort. Most of the names in the story were familiar to Bastide. He was glad to be out of it, away from the infighting. There was, after all, something to be said for working far from the capital.

Bastide sensed that someone was watching him. He glanced around the bar. He didn't have far to look. A young woman at a nearby table smiled when their eyes met. He returned to his paper. My God, he told himself, they're becoming more amateurish every day! No experienced *poule* would pick a policeman as a target. This one must be a real beginner. Bastide was vain enough to hope he could pass for someone else but an inspector of police. With his thick pepper-and-salt hair, his black mustache and broken nose, he could have been a rugby coach or a barman in one of Marseille's better hotels. Despite his stylish tweed suit, his profession seemed to have stamped him with an invisible label easily recognizable to anyone working the other side of the street. He caught the barman's eye and indicated he'd like another pastis. The neophyte hooker gave him another unctuous smile. He nodded to be polite and immediately regretted it. Seconds later, he looked up to find her sitting down at his table.

"*Bon soir,*" she said with false gaiety. "Will you buy me a drink?"

Bastide sighed and folded his paper. She was about twenty. She had a dimple at the corner of her mouth, and her hair needed washing. He took in her thin, ringless fingers, the cheap, flowered dress and the damp, rabbit-fur coat. She watched him, leaning forward expectantly.

"Listen, *petite,*" he told her, "you don't need a drink. I don't know you and I don't want to. Let me give you some advice. Never come in here again. This isn't your style. It would only mean trouble. Now, I suggest you leave before the barman throws you out."

She recoiled, surprised. For a moment her face was pale, then it flushed pink with anger. Her hands tightened on her imitation-leather handbag. "*Sale flic!*" she hissed, "you dirty cop!"

"Bravo," Bastide commented laconically. "At least you're learning. Now . . . go."

She left a cloying cloud of cheap perfume in her wake.

"Problem, Inspecteur?" The barman served his pastis and waited for an answer.

"Who was she?" Bastide asked.

"Never seen her before," the barman told him, wiping the table.

"She obviously doesn't have a sponsor," Bastide said, "or she wouldn't be in here."

"That's the way it is now. Free lances everywhere. A lot of them from the North."

"Fools," Bastide said. "Don't they know how dangerous it is?"

The barman shrugged. "Eh," he said, "what can one do?"

Bastide glanced at his watch. It was almost eight and he was hungry. He'd have to leave soon if he expected to find the *plat du jour* at La Mère Pascal still on the menu. He didn't look forward to walking along the quai in the steady drizzle, but La Mère Pascal was near his apartment. Janine Bourdet was in Morocco for a short holiday with her companion, the aged Monsieur Théobald Gautier, so Bastide would have to eat alone. He finished his pastis, pulled on his trench coat and nodded good-bye to the barman. The Vieux Port was covered by a sifting gray haze. The calm, black water lapped at the stone landings and the moored excursion boats. There wasn't much traffic. He didn't have to wait for a green light to cross the street.

He reached La Mère Pascal in five minutes. He entered, and Dominique told him she'd saved a plate of *pied et paquets* for him. It was one of his favorite dishes. He hung up his coat, sniffing the odor of the sauce that would cover the succulent sheep's trotters in their envelope of tender tripe.

"*Alors*, Roger," Dominique said, pushing her thick black hair from her forehead with the back of her hand, "a small pastis?"

"Yes, please."

Dominique was one of Marseille's best cooks. Her figure proved it. Bastide remembered her as a young Sophia Loren helping her mother in the kitchen. Since her mother had died, she'd taken charge of the restaurant and managed to please even the most difficult of the old regulars. Now Dominique's magnificent curves had become positively pneumatic. Bastide asked after Georges, Dominique's husband. Georges was ill.

"It's the weather," she said, shaking her head. "A filthy time. They're having better weather in Lille!"

Bastide found his regular table at the rear of the restaurant facing the door. Jean, an elderly, ponderous waiter, brought him a half bottle of red wine from Bandol and poured a glass with a shaking hand. Bastide asked for an endive salad to follow his pied et paquets. The restaurant was almost empty. The skipper of one of the Spanish trawlers lingered over his coffee. An angular couple with an accent that Bastide decided was Belgian were working their way through a large tureen of bouillabaisse, and Bastide recognized a local ship chandler who was spooning down portions of Dominique's rich chocolate mousse.

His pied et paquets arrived, steaming hot, swimming in a thick sauce flecked with pepper. Jean brought him some bread and he began to eat, savoring the delights of Dominique's cuisine.

Things had been quiet lately. A case on the docks had kept him busy in the fall. Overenthusiastic strong-arm tactics by the enforcers of a protection racket had left a longshoreman beaten to death. Bastide and his Corsican assistant, Barnabé "Babar" Mattei, had found the normally simple case very complicated. They'd had to move through a morass of obstacles thrown in their path by both management and the unions. No one wanted trouble on the waterfront, and one man's death was easily shrugged off to keep things on an even keel. Luckily for Bastide, a paid informer had finally earned his money and they'd picked up the murderer in Draguignan—a small, mousy man who looked as if he'd have trouble killing an ant.

Bastide broke a piece of bread and dipped it in the sauce. Chewing, he looked out at the street. The drizzle seemed to be dissipating. He pondered a constant worry: the pressure of the gangs from Nice who wanted to move in on some of the Marseille rackets. It was primarily the province of the antigang people, but if the Niçois ever made their move, his homicide section would have its hands full.

Jean shuffled over to take away his empty plate and serve the salad. Bastide sprinkled a bit more vinegar from a pressed-glass cruet into the mustardy dressing before eating the crisp endive.

When he'd finished, he leaned back in his chair and took a cigar from his leather case. He snipped off the tip with a small metal cutter and lit the cigar. It was a Cuban Larranaga. He'd been smoking now for a month. During the war in Algeria, he'd smoked strong, army-issue cigarettes. He'd given them up when he'd entered the police. Now he'd decided that a few cigars a day wouldn't affect his health. The promotion he'd received after breaking the McCallister case had made cigars an affordable indulgence.

"*Oh là là!*" Dominique chided him from behind the bar. "We now have a capitalist client!"

Bastide prepared to reply but stopped, his mouth open. "Babar" was pushing through the door, his broad bulk encased in a gray overcoat, a dark wool cap pulled low over his eyes. Mattei removed his coat and cap, hung them on a rack and sat down at Bastide's table. Bastide frowned.

"Well?" he asked.

"Sorry, but we've got a stiff. In Aix."

Bastide eyed the damp patches on Mattei's blazer where the rain had soaked through his cheap overcoat.

"Dominique," Bastide called over his shoulder, "two cognacs, please."

He waited till they were served before talking. "Let's have it," Bastide said.

"A student. A girl from one of the American institutions at Aix. Guignon called after looking things over. They found her in the shower of her apartment. Stab wounds, probably an ice pick. She shared the place with a roommate . . ."

"Male or female?"

"Female."

Bastide put his cognac down and signaled Mattei to continue.

"Guignon said things were in an uproar. Students crying, professors panicking, everyone running in circles."

Mattei smoothed his thick sideburns and ran his hand through his curly black hair. He took a gulp of his cognac before speaking again. "It's the Willy-ton University group," he explained, having trouble pronouncing the name.

"Any leads?"

"No. Guignon said he was having a hard enough time keeping people calm. I understand the Rector's Office of Aix-Marseille is not happy at all. They've asked Guignon to be discreet."

"Discreet? With a murder? They're living in another century."

Mattei agreed. He looked over Bastide's shoulder toward the bar. He was a handsome Corsican with a weight problem. His bulk in no way affected his self-esteem as a ladies' man. Dominique sensed his attention and returned his smile.

"That Dominique," Mattei said, "is *some* woman!"

"Yes," Bastide agreed, "there's a lot of her."

"I like a bit of flesh. The skinny young ones on the topless beaches, they—"

"Babar!" Bastide cut him short. "What did you tell Guignon?"

"I told him to hold tight and we'd be there soon."

"Good. I'd like to talk to these people while they're still upset. A night's sleep will cloud their memories and bring second thoughts."

"I'll have to call my wife," Mattei replied, unenthusiastically.

"Go ahead. I'll get my coat."

Bastide paid his bill and said good night to Dominique. He walked to the door and waited for Mattei to make his call. There shouldn't be much traffic on the *autoroute*. They'd be in Aix in a half hour. Bastide tapped the .38 detective special in the hip holster under his jacket. He didn't like carrying a *petard*, but since he'd been wounded by a gunman during the McCallister case he'd begun carrying again.

Dr. Ronald Gregg sat by the fireplace in the dining room of Willington House with a glass of straight bourbon in his hands. Marcia Chappel was pouring herself a sherry at the sideboard. The tables were still laden with trays of hors d'oeuvres, half-empty champagne bottles and dirty glasses. When Jean Bates had returned to tell of Ginnie Feldman's murder, she'd been incoherent with shock. Then Hank Castel had arrived accompanied by a police detective. After an hour of questioning, the detective had left. The Bates girl was now sleeping upstairs under sedation, and all the guests had gone off, buzzing with conjecture.

"My God," Gregg murmured, staring at the fire. "Why did this have to happen?"

Marcia Chappel put her glass down on the mantelpiece and turned her back to the fire. "It's terrible," she said, "that poor girl."

Gregg drank some bourbon, grimaced and shook his head. "Our whole program could be compromised," he said. "Two years of work down the drain."

Marcia Chappel frowned. "What did you say?"

"I said," Gregg replied testily, "that this stupid scandal could mean the end of the Willington program in Aix."

Marcia Chappel finished her sherry with one gulp. "You callous bastard," she said slowly before walking out of the room.

Dr. Gregg was ready for bed. He had just taken off his shoes when the doorbell rang. He cursed, slipping them back on, and hurried downstairs. The bell chimed insistently. He was prepared to greet his visitor sharply until he opened the door. The unspoken authority of the two men caused him to hesitate.

"Yes?" he said, looking from one to the other.

"Inspecteur Principal Bastide and Inspecteur Mattei," Bastide explained.

"Well," Gregg said, "it is very late and I've already spoken with Detective Guignon."

"We know. You are Dr. Ronald Gregg?"

"Excuse me, I didn't introduce myself. I am Dr. Gregg." He hesitated. "Won't you come in?"

"Our credentials," Bastide said, showing his identity card. Mattei followed suit. "We are with Homicide . . . Marseille. We will be handling this case."

"I see," Gregg said, leading them into the sitting room. "Please sit down. Ah, would you like a drink . . . or coffee?"

"No, thank you." Bastide watched Gregg. He noted the movements of his hands, his eyes, the way he spoke, the way he listened. "We won't keep you long," he said. "Tell us about the victim."

"Ah, she appeared to be a good student. She seemed bright . . . and polite. A good family. You see, we screen our students carefully. I know of no reason . . ." Gregg shrugged and his voice trailed off.

"Her personal life?"

"I'm afraid I can't be much help. These students are adults. They are here to study and learn. We do our best to see that things go smoothly . . . that they have a profitable year. Unless there is a real problem, we don't interfere in their personal affairs."

"Tomorrow we would like to look at her dossier. Everything you have on the girl."

"Of course. I'll see that Miss Chappel prepares it for you."

Mattei had been examining the room. "You had a party tonight?" he asked.

"Yes, a reception for Madame de Rozier, the dean of foreign students. You undoubtedly know her."

"We don't," Bastide replied, "but we will. Tell me, did Mademoiselle Feldman have a liaison of any kind?"

"Once again, I'm afraid I can't help. I've only seen her a few times since she's been here. Her roommate, Jean Bates, may be able to answer that question."

"Do you have any suspicions? Did any particular person come to your mind when you learned of the girl's murder?"

Gregg seemed surprised by the question. "Of course not," he said, a hint of anger in his voice. "No suspicions at all. I'm sure it was someone we don't even know."

"Why do you say that?" Bastide asked.

"As I explained, the students are carefully selected. My staff members are well-known, trustworthy academics. There's never been a murder at Willington University, not even an assault, and certainly no trouble of any kind here."

"Could we ask your Mademoiselle Chappel to supply us with a list of faculty members, employees and students tomorrow?"

"She'd be glad to." Gregg tried to suppress a yawn but failed. It was almost midnight.

"Where can we find Mademoiselle Bates?"

"At this hour?"

Bastide nodded. "Murders tend to keep people awake. I am sure the Bates girl follows the pattern. It is best for us to see her tonight . . . if only to gain a little time."

"She's asleep upstairs. The doctor gave her pills. Miss Chappel is staying with her. I'm afraid she won't be able to answer any questions tonight."

Bastide stood up. "Very well," he said, "I would appreciate it if you ask your students and staff not to leave Aix for any reason. As Monsieur Guignon may have told you, Mademoiselle Feldman's apartment has been sealed. No one, not even her roommate, can enter it . . . without a police escort."

"I see."

They walked to the door. Mattei looked longingly at a tray of uneaten hors d'oeuvres as he passed the table. He was hungry, but he dominated the temptation to help himself.

"Good night, Dr. Gregg," Bastide said. They all shook hands. When the door shut behind them, Mattei turned up the collar of his overcoat. "He's a cool one," he commented. "Dry as a squeezed lemon."

Bastide glanced up at the sky. The high clouds had opened. A winter moon illuminated the remaining bits of snow.

"Do you think he's notified the American consulate in Marseille?" Mattei asked.

"I don't know. Probably not. We'll pass it on to the Préfecture when we get back to the office."

"The poor family," Mattei commented as they walked to his battered Mercedes.

"I'm not going to like this case," Bastide told him. "Academics bore me."

"That," Mattei murmured, "makes two of us. Come on, before we leave I'll buy you a hot rum."

"No. I want to see the late Mademoiselle Feldman. Then we'll have the rum."

Mattei nursed the engine of his Mercedes into life while Bastide sank low on the seat beside him. He was thinking about death. He'd been familiar with violent death long before he'd come to the police. As a young parachutist in Algeria he'd seen enough blood and human destruction to last a lifetime. Once over the initial shock, he'd hardened himself, as everyone had, to the point where the sight of a shattered corpse, a dislocated mass of bone and flesh, became a natural part of the environment. But no matter how inured he became, he'd been continually surprised to see what jagged bits of metal and high explosives could do to the complex machinery of the human body. Now, after years of work in Homicide, he had the uneasy feeling that his hard carapace was softening. Murders were so personal, so seemingly unnecessary, they tended to make him angry. This was an unprofessional, dangerous attitude, but there didn't seem to be much he could do about it.

"You all right?" Mattei asked, piloting them around the Place Général de Gaulle and heading toward the morgue. "I'm having the heater repaired. Should have it next week."

Bastide sat up. "You've been talking about that heater for two years," he grumbled.

"You think there'll be someone at the morgue this late?" Mattei asked.

"They're supposed to have a night service."

"You're an optimist."

The morgue was ominously dark and quiet when they pulled to the curb. The slamming of the Mercedes' doors echoed along the empty street.

"Let's try the service entrance," Bastide suggested. They walked to the rear of the old building, the thick frost crunching under their steps.

"There's a light." Mattei pointed to an upper window. "I'll ring the bell." He leaned on the bell and they could hear it ringing inside. *"Putain!"* Mattei cursed. "If someone's in there, they sleep very soundly."

"We'll have to call Guignon from a café."

"Wait, I hear something. Someone is coming."

A light went on just inside the door. Bastide could see the white-coated attendant through the window. The man paused, shading his eyes in an effort to see out into the darkness, smoothing his unkempt hair with his other hand. "Who is it?" he demanded.

"Inspecteur Bastide and Sous-Inspecteur Mattei, Police Judiciaire, Marseille," Bastide replied. "Open up. We've got business."

They waited impatiently as the door was opened.

"Salut," Mattei said, flashing his identity. Bastide didn't bother showing his.

The attendant blinked at them in the harsh light. His eyes were puffy with sleep. "Who would you like to see?" he asked them.

"The Feldman girl."

"Ah, *l'Américaine!* Follow me."

He led them through two sets of swinging doors and along the white-tiled corridors to the storage area. The morgue reeked of a sweet-smelling disinfectant. An old policeman, an amateur philosopher, had once told Bastide that morgues had a subtle, hardly identifiable odor caused by the vacuum of human life. Mattei had a more down-to-earth theory. He said they were no more than well-scrubbed butcher shops with an abundance of private meat lockers.

They were led into the storage area. The attendant, wider awake now, whistled his way along the double tiers of large metal drawers, glancing at the labels. "Here she is," he said, rolling the drawer out easily. "Do you want some coffee?"

"No, thanks," Bastide replied.

Ginnie Feldman lay on her back. She was covered by an opaque plastic sheet. There were crystals of ice in her matted hair, her nostrils and on her lips. Her right arm was slightly bent, the hand raised above her thigh.

"Let's see the wounds," Bastide said.

Mattei pulled back the sheet. They were both silent for a moment, looking at the young body.

"Someone did a job on her," Mattei sighed. "No doubt about that."

The exit wounds showing on her throat and chest were swollen and raw, like burst boils. The blood had turned a bluish black from the cold.

"Let's have a look at her back," Bastide suggested, turning to the attendant. "We'll leave that to you."

The attendant slipped one arm under the trunk, the other under the thighs, and shifted the corpse onto its side. Bastide and Mattei bent closer, examining the entry wounds.

"Ice pick," Mattei commented.

"I'm not sure," Bastide said. "Look! Whatever the blade, it exited on almost every thrust. Too long for an ice pick."

"I've seen long picks in icehouses, where they work with large hunks of ice."

"Maybe."

Bastide lifted the hair at the back of the neck, dislodging a fall of ice crystals. *"Eh ba!"* he said. "Look at this. Probably the killing blow. At the base of the skull. Directly into the brain." He lifted the hair on the forehead, searching for an exit wound. He examined the top of the skull, pushing the stiff, icy hair aside. Nothing. He brushed his hands together and stepped back.

"Any sign of sexual molestation?"

"No, but she wasn't a virgin."

"All right," he told the attendant, "you can put her back."

The attendant settled the corpse effortlessly, as if he were handling a giant articulated doll.

"There you are, *ma belle,*" he murmured, replacing the sheet. "Would you sign the visitor's register?" he asked.

They walked back through the corridors to a small office near the front door, signed the register and said good night to the attendant. It took Mattei five minutes to start the Mercedes. They forgot about the hot rum. It was one o'clock before they swung onto the *autoroute* for Marseille.

Mattei lit a Gauloise cigarette and exhaled, filling the front seat with pungent smoke. "The poor parents," he commented. "She was a pretty little thing."

Bastide leaned back and shut his eyes. It would be a busy day. Even fifteen minutes of sleep before they got back to the office would be worthwhile.

CHAPTER II

Professor Pierre Costin, the director of the Willington University French Language Program, did not like Americans. He had managed to hide his attitude well. As his students filed out of the drafty classroom, he felt a special wave of resentment. Louts and bitches all of them, he thought. If he were not paid so well he would have left. He often comforted himself with that thought, but he also knew it was untrue. He had come to Willington because of his past, a past that any French teaching establishment would question.

He snapped his books shut and gathered them up as the last student disappeared from sight. A tall, cadaverous man with a gleaming bald pate, Costin considered himself the consummate intellectual. He had been a Communist in his youth, then an anarchist. Now he was nothing. He read the progressive press and the left-wing magazines, but the zeal had gone out of his politics. He flicked off the lights and left the classroom, reflecting on his students. He estimated that three in the class of ten were making an effort. The rest were hopeless. Their atrocious accents infuriated him. He deeply resented their lack of respect for him.

The murder of the Feldman girl had distracted his class. The morning session had been a disaster. He nodded to a fellow professor and hurried along the corridor, eager to leave the old university building Willington had rented for their classrooms. He, too, was preoccupied by the murder. Murder meant police, police meant investigations and investigations could mean trouble.

It had been six years since the incident. The student in Toul had been a precocious seventeen, her young womanhood premature and budding. She'd been a good student, the type that remained after class to discuss political theory with her professor. He remembered her clearly, the tight jeans, her unconscious sexuality and, above all, her lips. She'd come by his apartment to return a borrowed book and stayed for a glass of port. It was springtime, and a shaft of sunlight from his open window had shone through her cotton blouse, outlining her young breasts as she sat on his divan. She'd repeatedly licked the sweet wine from her lips with her tongue. His old demon had seized him. With the second glass, he'd jokingly talked of his erotica collection. She'd insisted on seeing a volume. Feigning reluctance while gauging his every move, Costin had selected a modern Danish publication featuring color photographs of innumerable and varied couplings, done, he'd explained, "with taste."

The result had been beyond his wildest imagining. Every minute of that afternoon was still clear in his mind. They'd retained their professor-student relationship, with him teaching her everything he knew. Thinking of it excited him. Her clumsy willingness, her firm, unspoiled body, her rapturous response to his lovemaking and those lips, finally his and doing whatever he required.

Costin walked out onto the street and turned toward the Cours Mirabeau. He frowned, remembering the sequel to his Toul encounter. She'd come back three times. At their last rendezvous she'd brought a friend, a dark, thin girl who'd joined in, revealing an already developed expertise. The girls talked to a friend. His student's father heard of their tryst and stormed into the school demanding Costin's dismissal and prosecution. To avoid scandal, the director finessed an arrangement with the offended family, including free tuition for the girl and a promise that Costin would be blackballed throughout the French teaching community. Costin left Toul hurriedly to avoid a court appearance. A year later, he took a job teaching French in Algiers, where he exaggerated his revolutionary sympathies to impress his new employers.

He'd been very careful in Algeria. He'd left his erotica collection in France. It had been a difficult two years, relieved only by occasional visits to a young prostitute recommended by an Algerian colleague. When he'd come to Aix he'd been armed with a recommendation for the Willington position from a naïve American cultural officer he'd befriended in Algiers. A hopeless Francophile, the American had thought Costin a brilliant, witty example of French academia at its best. That recommendation and Costin's chilly hauteur had impressed Dr. Gregg. Costin had been given the job.

Costin walked into a small restaurant near the Hôtel de Ville and sat at his usual table. He found it hard to concentrate on the short, handwritten luncheon menu. His old demon had plagued him increasingly in the past few weeks. It particularly bothered him that the object of his thoughts and sexual fantasies had been the Feldman girl.

Bastide had slept for three hours. He'd pulled himself out of bed at 7 A.M., made some strong coffee and sliced and buttered a tartine. He'd sat at his dining-room table staring out at the Vieux Port while eating his breakfast. He'd put on a clean shirt and the same tweed suit. He'd taken a cab to the Hôtel de Police to get a head start on his paperwork. He was just finishing a short, preliminary report on the Feldman case when Mattei arrived, bleary-eyed and rumpled.

"*Salut*, Babar!" Bastide greeted him.

"*Patron*," Babar replied.

"Get us an official car for today. I've had enough of that German revenge you drive."

Babar smiled, picked up the telephone and called the police motor pool.

The cluttered office was cold. Only one of the wall heaters was working, and a crack in the window glass let in enough drafty air to neutralize its effect. The cleaning staff hadn't reached Homicide yet. The wastebaskets were overflowing; the display case holding the mementos of past cases was gray with dust. One of the fluorescent lights overhead was buzzing and flickering. Bastide cursed, completing his report.

"Why is it we never get proper service?" he asked as Mattei put down the phone. "I see the damn Narcotics Section has just had its ceiling painted. Our lights don't work, my desk must be twenty years old. Even the typewriters are relics."

"The assholes in Narcotics are glamour boys," Mattei replied. "Ever since *The French Connection*, they've been strutting like peacocks. What they want . . . they get. All the foreign visitors go to their office, not ours. Politics, nothing but politics."

The door swung open and a dour Commissaire Aynard stepped into their office. His thin frame seemed lost under his heavy top-coat. His dark felt hat sat low on his ears, and his pointed oxfords had an eggplant sheen to them.

"Good morning," he said without warmth. He looked at them through his rimless spectacles. "Don't get up on my account." Neither one of them had budged.

It was unusual for Aynard to drop in unannounced. Bastide expected the worst. He and Aynard did not get along. Aynard was a nitpicker and an *arriviste*. Since Aynard had come from Lyon to Marseille, he'd made life miserable for the Marseille staff. He didn't like Marseille or the Marseillais. The feeling was reciprocal. For the past month, Aynard's ulcers had kept him at home three days a week. Now he'd improved and returned to full-time duty.

"Bastide," Aynard intoned, "I was called at home this morning by the rector of the university. He is a friend of mine and he wanted me to know about the Feldman murder. I, of course, would have preferred to hear of it from you, but . . ." He made a gesture of despair.

"I've just finished the report," Bastide replied, indicating the papers on his desk. "I intended to have it on your desk before you arrived."

"Very well," Aynard said, "but I want you to call me from now on—"

Bastide's jaw hardened. "You told me two weeks ago that you didn't want to be disturbed for routine investigations."

"That was when I was unwell. Now I want to be notified. This is not a *routine* investigation. It concerns one of the largest universities in France, it concerns the death of a foreign student. Not an Arab or an African but an American. It could have unpleasant repercussions. It should be tidied up quickly. I've given the rector my word."

Bastide replied with his eyes fixed on the wall opposite him. He knew that if he looked directly at Aynard he might say something he'd regret.

"Commissaire Aynard, we have already interviewed some of the principals in the case. We are returning to Aix this morning. That is, if we are not kept here too long."

Aynard frowned and walked to the door.

"The rector has made Madame de Rozier the coordinator for the university in this matter. She is in charge of the foreign students in Aix and a most respected member of the academic community. I want you to speak to her today. Understood?"

"*Compris,*" Mattei responded quickly, realizing that Bastide was nearing his explosion point.

"Good," Aynard said, glancing at Mattei as if he'd just noticed his presence. "*Mon Dieu,*" Aynard commented on leaving, "this office is a pigpen!"

Bastide snapped the pencil in his fist and threw the pieces across the room.

"You'll have ulcers next," Mattei warned. "Don't let him upset you. The hell with him."

"He's the Commissaire and our boss."

"No one promised us an easy life."

Bastide collected the sheets of his report and signed it. "Here, friend," he told Mattei, "you deliver this to Aynard's office. If I saw the bastard right now I think I'd strangle him. Oh, send in Lenoir on your way out."

Bastide pushed his typewriter aside and brushed some cigar ashes off his desk. He decided he'd pay a quick visit to Fernand Boiteau when they got to Aix. Then he thought about Lenoir.

Jean Lenoir was an earnest young detective who had been passed over for promotion on two occasions. Mattei had taken him under his wing and was giving him one more chance. Bastide approved, particularly since Aynard seemed determined to get rid of Lenoir. It wasn't that Lenoir was stupid. He was simply a dreamer in a world of realists and cynics. Bastide looked up as Lenoir poked his head in the door.

"You asked for me, Inspecteur?"

"Yes, Mattei and I are going up to Aix again. I want you to do some checking for us. We're looking for firms that supply icehouses and freezer companies with tools."

"Tools?" Lenoir had an irritating habit of repeating his orders as if they were basically incomprehensible. He was a good-looking young man with bushy blond hair and a drooping, gunfighter's mustache, neither of which endeared him to Commissaire Aynard.

"Yes, tools. Cutting equipment and picks," Bastide said with exaggerated patience. "We think the Feldman girl was killed with an ice pick. A long one."

"A long one?"

Bastide was beginning to wish Mattei hadn't taken such a fatherly interest in Lenoir.

"*Putain!*" Bastide exploded. "Wash your ears out. We want to know if long ice picks are available on the market, where they're sold, where they're used in the Marseille-Aix region . . ." Bastide took a deep breath, trying to calm himself. "Look, Lenoir. I shouldn't have to draw it for you on a blackboard."

"On a blackboard?" Lenoir replied. "Oh no, certainly not, *Monsieur l'Inspecteur.*"

"*Eh bien,*" Bastide ordered, "get moving."

When Lenoir had left, Bastide walked to the grimy window and looked past the dome of the cathedral to the harbor and sea. The Mediterranean was slate gray, a color that never appeared on postcards. Two fishing boats were rolling in from a night's work, each escorted by a flight of weaving, dipping gulls. The day was starting badly. First Aynard and then Lenoir. He couldn't do much about Aynard, but perhaps he should do something about Lenoir. Not all people were cut out for police work. The sooner they realized it the better. He'd have to talk to Mattei. Perhaps they should encourage the young man to seek another career. Bastide pulled on his jacket, adjusted the holstered Colt and picked up his trench coat. It looked British but it wasn't. He'd found it at a Marseille department store during a sale. It had been made in Yugoslavia, and the lining was unraveling. He paused for a moment, thinking. Then he picked up the telephone and called the office responsible for the renewal of bar licenses in Aix to ask about the status of Boiteau's Cave des Compagnons.

It took them forty minutes to get to Aix through the heavy truck traffic. Mattei parked the police sedan illegally, half blocking a pedestrian crossing, and remained in the car. Bastide banged with the wrought-iron knocker of the Cave des Compagnons. He had to knock three times before the heavy wooden door was opened. Fernand Boiteau, the owner, blinked at him from the darkened interior. He said nothing.

"*Bon jour,* Fernand," Bastide said, pushing the door inward. "Heat up some coffee. Let's have a little talk."

Boiteau was a giant in black leather trousers and matching vest. He wore a red wool turtleneck. A silver chain hung from his thick neck. He stepped aside, allowing Bastide to enter. The Cave smelled of stale tobacco and rancid wine. A single orange bar lamp threw a sickly light over the vaulted stone ceiling. Bastide walked to the bar. He smiled when he saw the row of empty scotch bottles. A plastic funnel lay beside a heavy demijohn of amber liquid.

"Still bottling your own scotch?" Bastide asked. "You should sell your secret to the British. You'd save them a lot of time and money." He picked up a crudely printed label and read it aloud: " 'Highland Heather . . . bottled in Scotland.' Really, Fernand," he said, shaking his head, "you exaggerate."

Boiteau moved behind the bar. He still hadn't said a word. He switched on an electric burner and put a Silex of stale coffee over the heat. He rested his two huge, weight lifter's arms on the bar and sighed. It was more of a wheeze from deep in his chest. Boiteau's head was completely shaven. His dark eyes were expressionless under heavy eyebrows, his mouth a straight line.

"Well," Boiteau finally said in a surprisingly gentle voice, "what is it you want?"

"Fernand," Bastide replied, "you have strange clients. You know it . . . and I know it. Basically that is your affair. It only becomes mine when one of your woman haters gets physical. Five months ago it was that naughty Freddie. The one who did the mastectomy without anesthetic on that aging whore. A very bad thing. Last year, and I'm sure you remember, it was your visitor from London who used a straight razor on the twelve-year-old girl after she got off the school bus."

Boiteau sighed again.

"Very well," Bastide continued, "I won't waste more time. A young American student, a girl, has been murdered. I know you get the bottom of the university barrel in here on weekends. I want you to put out your feelers, to listen, to ask questions."

"How was she killed?" Boiteau asked.

"Stabbed. Something sharp and thin. Probably an ice pick."

"Horrible," Boiteau commented, turning his broad back to pour Bastide a steaming cup of coffee.

"Yes," Bastide agreed, "I'm sure it will keep you awake at night." He took the offered coffee, sipped it and grimaced. "Now," he continued, "I'll be honest with you. I have no leads or special suspicions. From what little I know of the girl, it doesn't look like a jealous lover. At this point it could be someone who does not like women. It was obviously a case of overkill. Naturally my thoughts turned to your clients."

Bastide put down his cup of coffee and walked to the door. "I'm counting on you," he said. "Oh . . . before I left the office, I checked on your license. It's up for renewal in two months. I don't suppose there'll be any problem."

When the door closed behind Bastide, Boiteau put his hands on his hips and defiantly stuck out his tongue.

Hank Castel couldn't get Ginnie Feldman out of his mind. He'd only been exposed to death in flower-filled funeral parlors. The chalk-faced, pink-lipped products of the undertaker's art had always seemed unreal to him, papier-mâché replicas on their way to permanent storage. The raw wounds in Ginnie Feldman's nude corpse had been both obscene and nauseating. He hadn't eaten much since finding the body. The coffee he'd had at breakfast seemed to have stuck at the back of his throat. Dr. Gregg had asked to see him at three. He was ten minutes late. He pushed open the door of Gregg's office and found Marcia Chappel on the telephone. She motioned for him to sit down and continued her conversation.

". . . I understand. Yes, we'll send someone to meet you at the airport. I know. Yes, it must be very hard. We'll make hotel reservations. What? Yes. Aix is near the airport; about twenty minutes away by car. We are all shocked, Mr. Feldman, and very, very sad. Please accept our condolences. No, we have no idea. I'd rather not go into details now, if you don't mind. You do understand? The police will explain all that. Yes. French police. All right. Until tomorrow. Good-bye."

She put down the phone and wiped her eyes quickly with a handkerchief. Marcia Chappel seemed to have aged overnight. Her

normally neat hair was uncombed, her eyes were red and her hand
shook as she poured some tea from the teapot on her desk.

"That was Mr. Feldman, calling from New York. My God! The
poor man still hasn't grasped what's happened. Can you imagine?
Your daughter is suddenly dead and you're thousands of miles
away. He'll never see her alive again."

Castel cleared his throat. "Dr. Gregg asked to see me," he said.

Marcia Chappel stared at him, her mind elsewhere. "What was
that?" she finally asked.

"I'm here to see Dr. Gregg."

"He isn't here. He had to call on the rector. He'd like you to pick
up the Feldmans when they arrive at Marignane tomorrow. The
police will probably be here most of the day and he just can't afford
to be absent."

Castel felt his stomach tighten. He'd found Ginnie. That should
be enough. Why should he face her parents? It was asking too
much. "I've got classes all day," he replied, angry with himself for
such a weak argument.

"I'm sure you can make them up," Marcia Chappel said reassuringly. "He wanted you to go, as he feels you're more mature than
the other students."

"Can't you go?" he asked. "It is basically an administrative problem."

Marcia Chappel seemed shocked. She looked down at her desk,
frowning. "Very well," she said in a brittle, spinster's voice, "we'll
have to find someone else."

Castel felt trapped. What do you say to grieving parents? Welcome to France? Do you point out the sights on the way to Aix? Do
you tell them how you found their daughter?

"Look, if you really need me, I'll go," he finally told her.

Marcia Chappel glanced at him quickly and looked away again.
"I would go, but I can't," she said. "I couldn't stand it." She sobbed
and covered her face with the handkerchief.

Hank Castel stood up, embarrassed. "When do they arrive?" he
asked.

"They've got an Air-Inter flight from Paris in the afternoon. I'll
let you know the exact time tomorrow morning. You can take Dr.
Gregg's car."

Castel nodded. "OK," he said, "I'll check with you tomorrow."

"Hank, we are grateful."

"No problem," he replied, pushing open the door. He stood for a minute in the empty hallway. "Son of a bitch!" he cursed under his breath before walking slowly back to his dormitory room.

Madame de Rozier was standing in front of the fireplace when Inspecteur Bastide was ushered into her office. The high ceiling, the heavy window drapes and the Empire furniture made her appear even smaller in the flickering light of the wood fire. She was wearing a blue Chanel suit and a gray silk blouse. Her black hair had the shape and consistency of an oversize toxic mushroom.

"Madame," Bastide said as he entered.

"Inspecteur Bastide," she replied, "I've been waiting for you. Commissaire Aynard called to say you'd be here today. This is all so distasteful. I trust we can end our business quickly. Do sit down."

Bastide sat on the *canapé* near Madame de Rozier's desk. When she sat down, her tiny feet barely reached the floor. That bastard Aynard is already interfering, Bastide thought.

Madame de Rozier spoke first. "Have you heard the radio this morning? It's disgraceful. They're speaking of the university as if it were a crime center. Where do they dream up such rubbish? I hope you and your men don't speak to the press."

"Madame," Bastide said seriously, "a student has been murdered. That is the fact we must recognize."

"I understand perfectly. However, we know nothing about this person. She was, after all, a foreigner. God knows what her background has been. Do you know more about her?"

"Not for the moment," he replied. He'd been sure Madame de Rozier was going to be difficult, but he had not realized how quickly he'd dislike her.

"Well, I hope you can get to the bottom of things quickly. Every minute that passes without results is bad for the university."

"Madame," he said, "what is your opinion of the Willington University's program here in Aix?"

She pursed her lips, her hands toying with a gold-handled letter opener. "It is a new program. Well thought out. It appears to be going well. Or, it did appear to be going well."

"And Dr. Gregg? What are his qualifications?"

"A perfect gentleman and a recognized academic. His grammar is impeccable but his accent is horrible. You know, the Anglo-Saxons have problems with our tongue."

"This Mademoiselle Chappel, what is her role at Willington?"

"Oh, she supervises the office. An administrator. She does have one failing."

"What is that?"

"She drinks. I have nothing against drinking in moderation, but she goes a bit far. I'm surprised that Dr. Gregg does nothing about it."

"You've seen her intoxicated?"

"Not really. But, believe me, I know the symptoms." Madame de Rozier lowered her voice, speaking confidentially. "My husband, the late Count de Rozier, had that failing."

"Madame, this is a standard question but it must be asked. Do you have any suspicion, any thought as to who might have been responsible for Mademoiselle Feldman's murder?"

Madame de Rozier sat back in her chair. "Monsieur l'Inspecteur, I can tell you truthfully that it is a mystery to me. Oh, we've had a few problems here in the past, but they were minor. Almost all of them caused by outsiders. I suppose the fate of that poor girl can be linked with the violence of today's youth. No respect, no traditions. They feed on the television, a sewer of violence and sex. What can one expect?"

"Is there anything you feel would be useful to me in this investigation?"

"Well"—she paused before continuing—"there are many immigrant workers in the *quartier*. You know, from North Africa. They are far from home and without women. I am, of course, not a racist . . ."

"Of course," Bastide replied, making an effort to hide the skepticism in his voice.

"Nevertheless, I would not discount the possibility that . . ."

"Yes?"

"That one of these people might be involved. You know, they are not like us."

Bastide suddenly recalled the Algerian Harki who had fought like a lion to save two French children during an FLN attack on a farm near Blida. He'd been captured by the Fellagha three days later and disemboweled alive. Bastide's patrol had found him still breathing. Bastide had administered the *coup de grâce*.

"No," Bastide said, "not like us at all." He had a sudden desire to get away from Madame de Rozier and breathe some fresh, clean air. "I shall be in touch with you, Madame," he said. "Thank you for your time."

"I hope your investigation moves quickly," she replied, rising to see him out. "In any case, I shall be in contact with my good friend Commissaire Aynard."

Janine Bourdet was waiting in Bastide's apartment when he got home. Her stay in Agadir had deepened her fading tan. She was wearing a sweater of white wool and gray slacks. Her black hair was short. Her wide, sensuous mouth glistened with a new lipstick. She rushed into Bastide's arms and they kissed. Holding Janine again, even after a short absence, was a thrilling experience. He pushed her away gently.

"You look wonderful," he told her. "Morocco agreed with you."

"It was nice. A three-star hotel, good food and wine. Nothing to do but lie in the sun."

Bastide took off his jacket, unclipped the holstered revolver from his belt and put it in a drawer of the commode. "And Monsieur Gautier," he asked, "is he well?"

It was a stock question. Part of a ritual. Monsieur Théobald Gautier was an aged Marseille industrialist. Janine had been his mistress for six years. At the death of his wife she'd become his "companion." Gautier was an understanding man. He was generous with Janine, allowing her a considerable amount of independence. When Bastide and Janine had first met, three years earlier, during a prefectural reception, she'd demonstrated her independence by spending the night at Bastide's apartment. At first Janine's status had bothered him, but he'd learned to live with it. As time passed, they argued less and spoke of Monsieur Gautier as if he were an aged uncle. The only person their liaison seemed to displease was Commissaire Aynard.

"Monsieur Gautier is fine. His gout troubles him, but he's going off for a cure soon."

"Good."

Janine walked into the kitchen. He watched her as he unbuttoned his shirt cuffs and took off his tie. She had a surprisingly small waist. It accentuated her well-rounded figure. Bastide felt the familiar excitement of being close to her.

"It's almost eight," Janine said over her shoulder. "I didn't start anything, as I didn't know what you wanted. I did buy a large can of cassoulet."

"A can?" Bastide asked critically. He prided himself on his cooking. Tinned food had no place in his kitchen.

He followed her, walked past the butcher's block table, and reached under her arms to clasp her large, firm breasts. "There are four stuffed quail in the refrigerator," he whispered, kissing her neck. "We can have them . . . later."

She turned slowly, smiling. "I think Monsieur l'Inspecteur needs a woman."

"Just you, Janine," he replied.

He helped her out of the sweater and she took off her bra. "You've been sunbathing topless again," he said, kissing each nipple tenderly. Her dark eyes were alive as she helped him take off his shirt. Suddenly she clasped his shoulders and kissed him hard. When they separated, Bastide looked surprised.

"I *do* need a woman," he said, "but you're acting as if you need a man."

She unbuckled his belt without replying.

"*Bon sang!*" he swore, "what is this? Come, let's go to the bedroom."

"No," she replied, slipping out of her pants. "I'm fed up with silky bedrooms and soft mattresses."

"In my kitchen?"

"Yes, in your precious kitchen."

Her obvious desire and his own excitement settled the argument. With the reassuring thought that only a passing pigeon could see into his kitchen window, Bastide plunged into their love-making with enthusiasm.

He ran his hands slowly along her ribs; she turned her head to give him a long, deep kiss.

"You know," she finally said, "making love in the kitchen has certain disadvantages."

"Oh?" he questioned.

"My *nicbons* are covered with bread crumbs from your chopping block."

Laughing, they disengaged slowly and she sprinted for the bathroom.

"You," he called after her, "have one of the most beautiful behinds in Provence."

Later they sat side by side devouring the grilled quail with their fingers and drinking a bottle of Côte du Rhône. A single, large candle flickered on the table, throwing shadows over the copper pots. Bastide was wearing a dark robe and Janine was wrapped in a large towel that kept slipping off her shoulders.

"I have some good goat cheese," he told her, "and another bottle of this wine."

"I could have eaten more little birds," she said.

"Insatiable!"

"Perhaps. We'll see later."

"I have to leave early tomorrow," he said regretfully.

"A heavy case?"

"A sad one."

"Tell me."

"A young girl murdered in Aix. An American student." He pushed aside his plate and reached for a cigar. She watched him, still eating but suddenly solicitous.

"It bothers you?"

"Oh no, you know me better than that. I deal in cold meat. If each case bothered me it would be time to quit."

Janine put down what was left of her quail and reached out to touch Bastide's cheek. "Ah, *le dur*, the tough one," she said. "Don't tell me any lies. I can see this case is different. Was she pretty?"

He lit his cigar and blew a spiral of smoke toward the ceiling. "Yes," he replied, "she was."

"I see."

"No," he told her, "it isn't that, or the fact that someone stabbed her many more times than was necessary, or that we have no real leads. It's just that I don't look forward to tomorrow. Her parents will be here and I'll have to speak to them."

"Enough," Janine said, rising from the table, pulling the towel tightly around her. "The office is closed tonight, the bordello is opened! Agreed?"

Bastide chuckled. "Correct," he said. "We can have our last course in the bedroom . . . unless you object?"

Janine bared one full breast in the candlelight, examining herself carefully. "No objections," she said, "I've had enough bread crumbs for tonight."

The Feldmans were not at all what Hank Castel had expected. Without realizing it, he'd scanned the debarking passengers looking for a stereotypical Jewish couple. He realized now how his mind had been relying on old images, even prejudices. He'd pictured sad-eyed parents whom he'd have to comfort and guide like lost children through the baggage-pickup process. He'd been waiting for the creatures of his imagination when Mr. Feldman had tapped him on the shoulder to ask if he was there to meet them.

Castel smiled, remembering his surprise, and poured more beer into his glass. Fred Feldman had towered over him. With his brush-cut gray hair, he'd looked more like a former professional football player than a grieving father . . . until he'd noticed Feldman's eyes. They were blue and sad, focusing somehow on the past even when he looked directly at you. Mrs. Feldman, a large woman wearing a mink coat and diamonds, had been silent. She'd remained hidden behind her dark glasses. Only when he'd left them at their hotel had she spoken to thank him. It had all been civilized and low-key. They'd only mentioned Ginnie once, when they'd crested a hill to see Aix bathed in a bright winter sun.

"Ginnie must have loved it here," her father had said, and the remark had hung in the subsequent silence like an epitaph.

Castel was unwinding on the terrace of the Café Grillon. It was the first time in weeks the sidewalk terrace had been filled with customers. He ordered another beer from the busy waiter and buttoned the collar of his leather jacket. There was a chill in the air despite the sun. Since Ginnie's murder, he'd found himself playing detective. He'd been forcing himself to search his memory for any indication, any person, phrase or action that might be linked to her death. He'd been questioned by Sous-Inspecteur Mattei from Marseille. He'd been surprised how true the old clichés were. It had been like a film. Mattei had acted gruff and friendly, jovial and grim. The questions seemed to have come from some police manual. He'd done his best to cooperate, but the more questions he failed to answer, the more he sensed Mattei's suspicion. It wasn't obvious, but he could feel it. For the first time, he realized how an innocent person might be trapped by the wrong word or reaction. It had been a sobering experience.

He spotted Jean Bates before she saw him. She was walking down the Cours Mirabeau alone, resplendent in a baggy, pink knit sweater, tight jeans and a long gray scarf. Her blond hair was tucked under a black velvet cap, and he could see her squinting at the terrace, trying to locate a familiar face. He reached for the copy of *The International Herald Tribune* he'd bought earlier, hoping to hide behind it, but he was too late. She waved and wiggled her way toward him through the maze of occupied chairs and tables.

"Hi, Hank," she greeted him. "Buy a girl a coffee?"

"Hello, Jean. Sure. Sit down."

He hadn't seen her since the night they'd found Ginnie together. She'd been under a doctor's care and she looked awful. Her bouncy attractiveness seemed to have faded. He looked at her more closely and confirmed his first impression. She was high as a kite. Her brown eyes were dull, her movements languid and she smiled at everything and everyone. He ordered a coffee for her when the waiter brought his beer.

"Do you feel better?" he asked.

Her reply was another smile, a long pause and a question. "What?"

"I asked how you feel."

"Oh, great, super. I feel great, Hank."

"You starting classes again?"

"Sure," she said, drawing out the word and ending it with another vapid smile.

"I, ah . . . I met Ginnie's parents today," he told her. "They just flew in."

"Hey, Hank, that's great," she replied. "Want a joint?"

"No, thanks, Jean. I've got my beer."

"Too bad. It's good stuff. Top quality."

He tried to change the subject. "Are you still planning to go to Paris for Christmas?"

"No. I want to go to Nice or maybe Rome. That'd be nice. Rome." She unbuttoned her sweater and closed her eyes to the sun. She was not wearing a bra under her blouse and her body seemed lumpy and formless.

"Know what I think?" she asked. "I think it's all shit!"

"What?"

"All this college crap. I'm out of it. Know what I mean?"

He didn't, so he said nothing.

"Like, Ginnie's out of it," she continued. "Way out. They bury her yet?"

He frowned. "No, there's a service tomorrow. Then she's going home with her parents."

"Going home? Hey, that's neat." She opened her eyes again. "Do Jews bury people or burn them?"

"I'm not sure. Like everyone else, I suppose."

She took a fat joint from her canvas handbag. Stray filler ends were hanging from the brown paper. She flicked her cricket lighter, inhaling deeply. A cloud of acrid smoke swirled over the table.

"Jesus!" Hank commented. "What is that stuff?"

"Hash. I get it from a Moroccan friend. He's studying geography."

"He ought to try horticulture." His weak attempt at humor failed.

"There's one problem," she said, releasing a residue of smoke from her nostrils. "They burn too fast. Listen." She held the joint to his ear. He could hear it crackling.

"Sounds like a forest fire," he commented.

"You're so right." She slumped lower in her chair and took another drag. "I talked to the cops," she said quietly. "That inspector, he was cute. Asked a lot of questions. What's his name?"

"Mattei. He questioned me, too."

"Trouble was, I was down, real down. I couldn't get my act together. Forgot to tell him something."

"Like what?"

"Like, she had a thing about that French professor. You know, the skinny creep."

"Costin?"

"Yeah. She thought he was something."

"What do you mean, 'had a thing'?"

"Oh, she talked about him. He gave her a book of French poetry to read. Said she was the only one in the class who'd understand it. I just remembered last night. What do you think?"

"About what?"

"Should I tell this Mat—"

"Mattei. I think you should. They need all the information they can get. Did Ginnie ever see Costin . . . out of class?"

"I don't know. She didn't talk much. A great roomie! I had to pump her for everything." She leaned her head against his shoulder. "I'm flying," she said, "and I've got the itch. Wanna make it?"

Castel glanced down at her. She smelled of hashish. There were flecks of dandruff on her cap. Making it with Jean Bates was the last thing in his mind.

"You're flying," he told her, "but I'm not."

"Okay, I get the picture. I'll just drift on. Other studs on the farm, you know."

She slung her shoulder bag and stood up. She hadn't touched her coffee. "You know what?" she said as if she were sharing an important secret, "I lost my goddamn contact lenses! No use going to class now."

"You're going to tell Mattei about Costin, aren't you?"

"Huh? Oh, I suppose so. Not that it makes any difference. Ginnie's dead." Tears welled up in her eyes as she dropped the smoking butt of her joint on the sidewalk.

"I hate this goddamn town," she announced loudly. The French students at a nearby table turned toward her. She smiled at them and walked off swinging her hips in a sad imitation of a fashion model.

Castel tried to concentrate on the front page of his *Herald Trib-*

une. He couldn't. He was thinking about Professor Costin. It was hard to see him as a possible murderer. Jean Bates was certainly not a reliable source. She could be saying the same things about him. But Costin was strange. Innocent or guilty, he wasn't a very likable person. Castel folded his paper and prepared to pay his bill. He'd made up his mind. If Jean Bates didn't mention Costin to Mattei, he would.

CHAPTER III

The voice cut through the frigid air like a blade. It carried far over the din of passing traffic with a quality that caused passersby to pause, if only for a moment. The singer slumped over a guitar, his head moving from side to side in rhythm to the music, long blond hair shining in the sun. He'd taken over a public bench under the leafless plane trees on the Cours Mirabeau and seeded his open guitar case with a few one-franc coins to encourage donations. He had the face of a Nordic Christ: high forehead, prominent cheekbones and deep-set blue eyes.

Pedestrian traffic was light, but a young couple in jeans and leather jackets and a squat older woman leading an aged, overfed terrier had stopped to listen. Twenty feet away, an unshaven drunk with a puffy, bruised face and bloodshot eyes was shuffling to the music in a grotesque parody of ballroom dancing.

The singer didn't lift his head when Marcia Chappel dropped a five-franc coin into the guitar case and hurried on. She did not want to be late for Dr. Gregg's meeting with the Feldmans. He'd insisted on her presence, and she'd promised to be there. She glanced over her shoulder at the blond troubador. She'd seen him before, but she'd never given him anything. She wasn't quite sure why she had now. Something about his voice, his aura of vulnerability, had attracted her. She turned off the Cours, walking toward the Willington house, wondering how her analyst would have interpreted her gesture. She'd been out of analysis since she'd left for France, but she often thought of Dr. Sichburn. She buttoned her tailored wool jacket against the cold, thinking that Sichburn would have worked his way slowly but methodically back to his favorite theory: She was a born mother with no children. Her need to mother someone was only expressed in relation to younger males.

Her real urge, therefore, was not to mother anyone, but to seek sexual fulfillment in the arms of a son-lover.

Marcia Chappel was still frowning at the memory of Dr. Sichburn's theory when she pushed open the door of the Willington house. A female student working part time in Gregg's outer office stopped chewing gum long enough to tell her that the Feldmans had arrived. She knocked and entered.

Mr. Feldman stopped talking and stood up when he saw Marcia Chappel. Mrs. Feldman was still wearing her dark glasses. Dr. Gregg introduced them.

"I was just saying," Mr. Feldman continued, "that we appreciate what you've done for Ginnie and for us." His voice was deep and controlled. Mrs. Feldman seemed to have found something of interest in the design of the Oriental rug under Dr. Gregg's desk.

"We want to help as much as we can while we're here."

Dr. Gregg readjusted his glasses and cleared his throat. "I know how difficult this must be, for both of you," he said solemnly. "I don't have to tell you how shocked and sad we all are. I . . ."

Marcia Chappel watched Mr. Feldman as Gregg spun a web of appropriate clichés. She'd examined Ginnie's dossier that morning and knew a little about her father. He'd graduated from Columbia and was now the vice president of a building firm in New York. He had the confident manner of a self-made man. As she watched him listen to Gregg, Feldman's expression changed from quiet attentiveness to anger. She looked quickly at Gregg, trying to warn him, but he was oblivious to the gathering storm.

Mr. Feldman held up his hand. Gregg paused, surprised. "Dr. Gregg," Mr. Feldman said slowly, "I don't want to be rude, but we'll get enough of that from our rabbi. Ginnie was our only child. We loved her very much." He paused to take a deep breath before continuing. "She was murdered here. Why or how I don't know. But I am going to find out. I want her killer punished. If necessary I'll come back to France. You see, we will bury our girl, but we won't bury this murder."

Dr. Gregg nodded gravely. "I understand," he replied. "Any father—or mother—would feel the same. I've arranged for the police to speak with you this afternoon. I must warn you that their questions may be painful. The French police are not known for their tact."

Marcia Chappel thought Gregg's words had a particularly hollow ring. She knew him well enough to decipher the problem. He was really thinking about what effect the prolongation of the investigation would have on the Willington program.

"Dr. Gregg," Mr. Feldman said, "we'll be ready to talk to the police at any time. We're going to have a cup of tea now. You can reach us at our hotel. Come along, Jane."

Mrs. Feldman rose like an automaton, nodded her good-bye and the couple left the office. Dr. Gregg sighed, shaking his head.

"I'm afraid the Feldmans will be a problem," he told Marcia Chappel. "I understand their grief, but he's so aggressive. I'd like you to be with them when they speak to Inspector Bastide. They'll need someone to translate and I think it's important for us to know what is said."

Outside, the Feldmans paused to choose a café. "What do you think?" Mr. Feldman asked his wife.

"About what, Freddie?"

"About this Dr. Gregg."

She shrugged. "I think I don't like him."

"Come on," he said, taking her arm. "Let's go over there. The café with the red awning."

"Freddie," Mrs. Feldman said quietly, "I want to see my little girl."

The sun was disappearing behind the Fort Saint Jean, and the apartment buildings along the Quai du Port were bathed in a rose light as Bastide laid out the ingredients for his meal. He was preparing a special treat for Babar and his wife. A friend from the Alpes de Haute Provence had brought him some beautiful venison chops. He'd put them in a marinade of vinegar, white wine, whole-grain pepper, thyme, bay leaf, parsley and onions for twenty-four hours. The chops were ready for sauteeing, dark red and succulent. He'd drained some blood from them to use in his *sauce poivrade* before submerging them in the marinade. He'd also dropped by La Mère Pascal on his way home to wheedle some *sauce coulis* from

Dominique. It was essential to the *poivrade*, and he didn't have the four or five hours needed to produce it.

He passed his hand inches above the heavy iron casserole. It was hot and ready. He dropped a hunk of butter into the casserole, gave it a quick shot of oil to keep it from browning too soon, and watched it melt and spread. When it was bubbling, he added a chopped carrot, a chopped onion and some fatty cuttings from the chops. He stirred the mix lightly with a wooden spoon before turning to his cutting board.

Wielding a sharp knife with professional dexterity, Bastide chopped two shallots and crushed a large clove of garlic with the flat of the blade. He removed the small green sprout from the center of the clove and discarded it. When the onion and carrot had taken on a bit of color, he added the shallots and garlic, threw in a bay leaf, a twig of thyme and a healthy pinch of crushed black pepper. He added a half glass of vinegar, shook the casserole and then poured himself a generous glass of pastis. It would take some time for the liquid to reduce. He walked to the kitchen window and looked out at the Vieux Port. He hadn't entertained the Matteis for months, and he'd felt like company. Mattei had jumped at the chance. Babar loved his children, but, each day, the six of them automatically turned his modest apartment into an echo chamber on their return from school. He also knew his wife needed a night out to preserve her sanity.

Bastide watched the evening traffic passing along the Quai. A police van roared by, klaxoning its way through the intersections. He frowned, remembering his interview with the Feldmans. The Chappel woman had acted as a translator. It had gone well, but Mr. Feldman bothered Bastide. He was too controlled, too businesslike. Perhaps Americans were like that. Mrs. Feldman had asked permission to visit the morgue. Bastide had not refused, but he'd exchanged a significant glance with the husband. Feldman had nodded his approval. It had been arranged. While Miss Chappel remained outside in the car, Bastide had accompanied them. The mother had run her trembling hands over the girl's face as if she expected her to awaken. The father had stood behind them in silence, his eyes fixed on what had been his daughter, his breathing audible in the stillness of the cold room.

Mrs. Feldman had then returned to the hotel, and Feldman, Miss Chappel and Bastide had gone to a café. The American ordered Armagnac for them before responding to Bastide's questions. His answers had given Bastide a better insight into Ginnie Feldman. She'd been a quiet girl. A romantic with high ideals who wanted to do something for the world. Her father remembered having to temper her enthusiasm with reality as she grew older. She'd always listened to him, he'd said, but he was never sure how much she really retained or if she agreed with his points. The few boyfriends she'd had were from the same mold. Mademoiselle Chappel had had some trouble translating the father's characterization of them as "knee-jerk liberals." She'd come up with "head in the clouds," a variation that puzzled Bastide and didn't please Mr. Feldman. Bastide remembered how nervous Mademoiselle Chappel had been. She'd downed her Armagnac like a Gascon farmer and accepted a second glass before the two men had finished their first. A strange woman, Bastide thought. Not unattractive, but definitely carrying a weight of problems.

Mr. Feldman had talked of his daughter as if she were still alive. She'd been planning a career in the American Foreign Service and was to take the examination once she'd finished college. When Bastide had asked if she'd been serious about any male friends, the father had shrugged. He obviously didn't know or didn't want to talk about it. Bastide remembered the morgue attendant's comment that Ginnie Feldman had not been a virgin. It was unbelievable how little some parents knew about their own children.

Then Mr. Feldman had started his interrogation. He'd asked Bastide about his methods, his police resources, his view of the case and even his professional experience. Mademoiselle Chappel had tried to deflect Feldman's questioning, but the American had been determined. By the time they'd parted, Bastide felt he'd been on the grill.

Bastide finished his pastis and turned back to the stove. He filled a glass with some Gigondas and poured it into the casserole. He opened a jar and poured out three thick cups of the *sauce coulis* Dominique had given him, stirring it into his mixture. He covered the casserole and reduced the heat, glancing at his watch. In an hour's time the *sauce poivrade* should be ready. It would then be a question of removing the grease, straining the sauce into a smaller pot for a few more minutes of boiling before mixing in the blood saved from the venison chops.

He reached for a *baguette* of bread and sliced it into rounds. The crumbs on the chopping block reminded him of his last rendezvous with Janine. He smiled, putting the bread in a serving basket. Janine wouldn't be joining them for dinner. She was attending a dinner party with Monsieur Gautier, one of those bourgeois ceremonials that brought the old families of Marseille together on Friday evenings over *soupe au poireaux* and a *gigot* of lamb served by temporary Spanish help.

He turned on the light and sat down at the kitchen table. The thought of Janine reminded him of Mireille Peraud, the other woman in his life. Madame Mireille Peraud, he corrected himself. After all, she was still married to the naval officer in Toulon. Jacques Peraud was not a bad type, but he was often away on official business or sea duty. Bastide and Mireille had been high school sweethearts. Then, without warning, she'd married Jacques, a young ensign, in Paris. Bastide's bitter deception had sent him into an army recruiting office, where he'd volunteered for service in a parachute regiment. It had all been long ago and damned childish. He'd learned the truths about life, death and revolutionary war in the rocky hills of Algeria while Mireille had entered the daily routine of a naval officer's wife.

Two years earlier, he'd discovered that the Perauds were based in Toulon. He'd seen them from time to time, at the Cercle Sportif in Marseille or at luncheons with mutual friends. At each meeting, he'd felt Mireille's interest in him. He was sure he could have had her with a little effort. But the Perauds had children and, although he sensed that Mireille was bored with her life, he'd hesitated. God knows she was even more attractive now. He leaned back in his chair, imagining her long legs, the blue eyes, the provocative stance and her manner of running her fingers through her thick, russet hair. He'd been tempted to accept one of her many invitations to lunch during Jacques's repeated absences. But something had held him back. It certainly wasn't out of respect for her marital status. He'd had some trouble with a *commissaire*'s wife in the past, but he didn't think it was fear of such complications. He wasn't sure why, but he had drawn an impassable line between them.

"*Eh, merde!*" he cursed, rising to go back to his cooking.

By the time Mattei and his wife arrived, Bastide had prepared a small dish of green olives in oil and thyme and a plate of roasted almonds to go with their apéritif. Mattei brought a bottle of red wine from Bandol as his contribution to the dinner. Marie Mattei kissed Bastide on both cheeks while her husband hurried to the bottles on the sideboard and poured himself a pastis.

"Don't you want a whiskey?" Bastide asked. "I bought a bottle of Johnny Walker yesterday."

Mattei shook his head. "No need to waste scotch on me. It's not my drink. Too much of a head the next morning."

"What would you like, Marie?" Bastide asked.

"A little vermouth," she replied, "with ice."

Mattei's wife was short and heavy. She'd evidently curled her dark hair and put on one of her best dresses for the occasion. The yellow silk was stretched to its limit by her ample figure. Bastide liked Marie Mattei. She was always in good humor no matter what family crisis she'd just faced.

"*Tchin'-tchin'!*" she toasted with a broad smile, raising her glass. "To a very good dinner."

Mattei raised his leonine head and sniffed. "Oh là là!" he said. "Something smells magnificent!"

"We'll let Marie be the judge," Bastide replied, pouring water into his pastis. "Here, have some almonds or olives."

They sat down around the low cocktail table and Mattei stretched his legs. He popped some almonds into his mouth. Marie Mattei glanced around her. She'd helped Bastide furnish the apartment in Provençal style when he'd first moved to Marseille. She'd found the old dining-room table of thick, bleached wood well off the tourist track in the small town of Meounes. His heavy battery of cast-iron cooking pots had been discovered, coated with dust and spiderwebs, in the same shop.

"It's too bad Janine can't be here," Marie said. "I haven't seen her for a long time."

Bastide smiled. "She asked me to say hello. But—"

Mattei sat up suddenly. "Before I forget," he said, "Commissaire

Aynard called after you'd left the office. That Madame de Rozier from the college wanted to know how our investigation was going. I said you'd see him first thing tomorrow. Told him you were out on the case."

Marie Mattei laughed, covering her gold-capped incisor with one hand. "Out on the case? If Aynard wasn't such an old woman, you could have said Roger was cooking for us."

"One other thing," Mattei recalled. "The young American, that Castel, telephoned from Aix to say he'd like to talk to me. What do you suppose is in his craw?"

"I don't know, Babar," Bastide replied, "but we'll find out tomorrow. For the moment . . . no more business." He gestured with his thumb toward the kitchen. "We'll concentrate on the venison tonight."

Lenoir was proud of himself. He'd found an ice pick that should satisfy Inspecteur Bastide. The young detective opened the paper bag he was carrying and put the ice pick on Bastide's desk. It had a heavy handle of light-colored wood. The round steel blade was twice the length of a normal pick. He was alone in the office, waiting for Bastide or Mattei. He sat down in Mattei's chair and opened his notebook. He'd bought the pick at a wholesale supply house in Marseille that provided tools to the ice and brewery industries. He'd noted the name of the establishment, the cost of the pick, its length and weight. He'd even discussed its use with the sales clerk, who'd told him more modern, mechanical cutting tools would soon make the long pick obsolete.

Lenoir fingered his drooping mustache and tried to think. Why would a murderer choose the pick as a weapon? It didn't seem practical. What murderer would even know such a tool existed? He wanted to volunteer a theory when his superiors arrived, but he found himself distracted by Mattei's wall display of nudes clipped from a wide variety of erotic magazines. Two voluptuous, thoroughly soaped women fondling each other under a shower was particularly troubling. Lenoir swung around in his chair, putting his back to the wall. He picked up the pick, balancing it in his hand. A rare flash of insight drove the soaped flesh from his mind. Someone in the business! That was it. A murderer who worked with ice. He leaned back in his chair and nodded. A few moments of thought and he'd narrowed the field of suspects considerably.

Mattei pushed open the door, took off his coat and frowned at Lenoir. It took a few seconds for Lenoir to realize he was occupying Mattei's chair. He jumped up.

"Good morning, Inspecteur," he said.

"*Salut,*" Mattei replied, hanging his coat on a wall hook. "What's that?"

"What's what?"

"In your hand!"

"Oh, that's the ice pick Inspecteur Bastide wanted."

Mattei took the pick and examined its length, remembering the wounds. "It could have done the job," he said, sitting down heavily.

"I . . . I think the pick tells us something," Lenoir ventured.

Mattei adjusted his holstered revolver so it wouldn't be against the chair's back and looked at Lenoir. "So? What does it tell us?"

"It's an indication . . ." Lenoir hesitated.

"Go on."

". . . an indication that the murderer probably worked with ice."

Mattei resisted the temptation to tell Lenoir Bastide had sent him after the pick with just that possibility in mind. He liked Lenoir. As dull as he was, the young *moustagache* kept trying. He laid the ice pick on his desk.

"Very good," Mattei said, trying to sound impressed. "I'll pass that on to Bastide. Now I'd like you to go down to the canteen and bring me some black coffee. I drank *marc* last night after dinner and my head's a bit delicate."

Lenoir pulled on his leather jacket. He paused at the door. "Anything to eat?"

"No," Mattei told him. "Definitely not."

Mattei had begun to read a report he'd drafted, when the phone rang. It was the Castel boy asking when he'd be able to see him. Mattei arranged an afternoon meeting at the Café les Deux Garçons in Aix. He put down the phone and glanced at the wall clock. It was almost ten. He decided to leave immediately. He had some checking to do with Sous-Inspecteur Guignon, and he could eat a *pan bagnat* and have a glass of wine for lunch near police headquarters in Aix. He scribbled a note about the ice pick and waited impatiently for his coffee, wondering where Bastide might be.

Bastide was upstairs in Commissaire Aynard's office, and Aynard was pushing a pile of newspapers across his desk toward him.

"As you can see," Aynard said, "the press is amusing itself with the Feldman case. They've made the killer into some sort of Fantomas who is outsmarting the police every step of the way. I had a call from the American consul general this morning. He asked about the case and offered his help."

"His help?" Bastide asked.

"Yes, I suppose he'd send us his FBI if he knew how little progress we've made."

"It's only been a few days," Bastide responded.

"I know. I'll tell you frankly, I am not at all concerned about the Americans and what they think. It's the university I'm worried about. If we can clear this up quickly, show it was probably an outsider who was responsible, I'd feel much better."

"Someone from the outside?"

"Don't be dense! Educators don't go around murdering students. It would be bad for their profession." Aynard bared his teeth, signifying an attempt at humor. "In the long run, the university's reputation will suffer. The dean has made that clear. So, once again, I ask you to make a special effort. If you need extra men, don't hesitate, I'll see you get them."

"Thank you, we're all right for the moment."

Aynard peered at him over his spectacles. "You're all right? With that gorilla Mattei and Lenoir the lucid? You need a bright young policeman on your team. Someone who can spread his wings and operate efficiently. Someone who can think. Don't be surprised if I make the decision for you one of these days and handpick someone from another section. Granted, your team did a good job on the McCallister case, but much of it was luck. We can't count on luck in this business."

Bastide rose from his chair. "If that's all, I'd better get back to my office."

"Yes, that is all, Inspecteur." Aynard began to riffle through a pile of invitations. "Wait," he called as Bastide reached the door.

"The newspapers. I want you to read them. You'll see what I mean."

Bastide returned and gathered up the newspapers, leaving Aynard to his social schedule.

Jean Bates hardly noticed the young man who sat down next to her on the bench. She'd walked the length of the Cours Mirabeau trying to get the fuzz out of her head. Her stomach felt like a convention of butterflies. She'd already lost what little breakfast she'd managed to swallow. She couldn't quite remember what had happened the night before, but she knew she'd been in someone's apartment. There'd been plenty of hash and pills. Her high had been cosmic. She had vague recollections of a large bed she'd shared with others. Sometime during the night two men had made love to her.

"Want a pear?" the young man asked.

"No, thanks," she said, trying to focus her eyes on his blurred figure.

"Fall sunshine is the best," he commented, propping a guitar case between his legs.

She blinked and smiled in his direction. He was taking visual form now. A thin, handsome boy with long blond hair and deep-set eyes the color of seawater.

"You American?" he asked.

"Yes."

"I had an American father," he told her, "and a German mother. You at the university?"

"Look, friend," she said, closing her eyes to forestall the dizzyness she knew was coming, "I don't feel too good, OK?"

"Didn't think you did. You're down in the deep depths this morning, right?"

Jean Bates nodded. He was good-looking, but she wished he'd go away.

"Here," he said, taking a small tin box from the pocket of his tattered army field jacket. "Take this and you'll be back on top of the world." He handed her a small blue capsule.

"I can't swallow anything."

"It goes down easy. I'll show you." He popped the pill, swallowed it with ease and smiled at her. "See? Come on." He shook the box under her nose.

She took a capsule, turning it in her fingers, watching its color shine in the sun. "This going to blow the top off my head?"

"No, it's real light duty. It'll just bring you back."

Jean Bates tilted her head and gulped it down in one, practiced movement. She smiled at her benefactor and nodded toward his guitar case.

"You a musician?"

"It keeps me eating."

"You're not a student?"

"No, I gave up that nonsense in Germany."

"What are you doing in France?"

"I came here to join the Foreign Legion."

"The Foreign Legion? Does that still exist?"

"Sure. Luckily, I talked to some young German legionnaires before I signed up. They changed my mind."

"So now you're a minstrel?"

"A what?"

"A minstrel, you know, a wandering musician."

"Yeah," he said, exaggerating the American pronunciation. "I like that. I'm a minstrel."

"Hey, you know," she told him, "I feel better. I think your stuff is working."

"It always does. So tell me about yourself. Are you a student?"

She began slowly, then speeded up as she felt a new surge of energy. She told him about her family, her decision to study French, her enrollment in the Willington program, her boredom in class and the shock of her roommate's murder. He listened, leaning toward her. She noticed the intensity of his eyes. He seemed to be methodically examining every part of her as she spoke.

She broke off her tale. "You got a problem?" she asked.

"No. Why?"

"Like, the way you're looking at me. You a weirdo or something?"

He laughed. "I don't know. What do you think?"

Jean Bates smiled. "You're different."

"Where do you live?" he asked.

"Not far from here. How about you?"

"Out at Le Tholonet. A French friend loaned me his cabin near Montagna Sainte Victoire. It's Cézanne country."

"Cézanne?"

"You know, the painter."

"Oh, yeah."

"You'll have to come out and visit me," he said. "It's really beautiful. How do you feel?"

"Much better."

"Can I buy you a sandwich?"

"Okay," she replied. "How about a hamburger at Le Quick?"

"Anything you say. What's your name?"

"Jean. How about you?"

He hesitated a few seconds, his blue eyes continuing the inventory of her body. "Just call me the minstrel. It's the best name I've ever had."

Mattei decided to run a detailed check on Professor Pierre Costin before he talked to him. Hank Castel had told him what Jean Bates had said. He didn't find the fact that Costin thought the Feldman girl a good student grounds for suspicion, and he wasn't sure where Castel's interests were. He'd just put down the phone after talking to police headquarters in Paris when it rang again. He recognized the voice immediately. "L'Escargot," one of Mattei's informers in the Endoume quarter of Marseille, was on the line. He spun out a voiceprint of slime that had earned him his name.

"Mattei," he oozed, "there's a warm one waiting for you at Loulou's. Could be one of the boys from Nice. I didn't want to get too close."

"Give me more," Mattei ordered. "A damn chambermaid could tell me as much."

"Easy, easy. I'm telling you the truth. If you don't get there soon, he'll be on his way to a gravel pit or doubling as fish food. Look, I'm on a café phone. I don't like it here."

"Hold it!" Mattei bellowed. "You hang up on me and I'll put you on ice for a few years. Now, where is he exactly; who chopped him and how?" Mattei could visualize L'Escargot, his bony head sunk between his shoulders, long strands of lank hair brushed over his balding skull and sweat beading his forehead.

"They tell me he's in the shithouse. The door looks like a Gruyère. I'll call you later from somewhere else."

Mattei cursed and hung up. Lenoir was working with the forensic people on another case, so he was stuck. He called the switchboard to give them his coordinates and asked for a uniformed backup. He checked the safety on his .38 and pulled on his wrinkled blue blazer. He'd have to hurry if he expected to find a body.

The Hôtel de Caire, locally known as Loulou's, was a block from the sea. Mattei parked his Mercedes and hurried along the narrow, dirty sidewalk to the front door. The two-story building seemed to sag forward over the street, its façade a collage of cracks and peeling ocher paint. The gray wooden shutters were closed tight. When Mattei tried the heavy door, he found it locked. He almost rang the bell but changed his mind and walked quickly to the tiny alley that led to the rear of the building. He unbuttoned his blazer to give quick access to his hip holster. It paid to be careful when dealing with gang killings.

As he walked into the refuse-filled yard, he could hear someone arguing inside. He stepped over some empty wine bottles, drew his .38 and kicked at the door. The sunlight through the doorway illuminated an unusual tableau. Loulou and three of her girls were standing over a man's body wrapped in plastic sheeting. It was lying on the hall rug, face down. The women turned, openmouthed, facing Mattei, surprised by his unexpected entry.

"*Tiens,*" Mattei commented, holstering his revolver, "what have we here? Spring cleaning already?"

Loulou avoided the question by coughing. Her girls backed away from the corpse. They were dressed in flimsy miniskirts, cheap satin blouses and high-heeled slippers. Loulou's skinny frame was belted into a quilted purple housecoat; her dyed hair shown yellow in the light. She drew deeper on the cigarette hanging from the corner of her mouth and frowned at Mattei.

"The cowboys still around?" Mattei asked, glancing up the stairs.

"No," Loulou rasped, before coughing again. One of the girls retrieved a heavy breast that had escaped from its satin confinement.

Mattei removed some of the plastic sheeting with his toe and bent over the dead man. "*Pardi!*" he said, examining the carnage. "Did they use an elephant gun?" Holes as big as a fist had been punched in the man's back. Mattei could see bits of white bone and pink lung tissue through the ripped cloth of the suit jacket.

Loulou cleared her throat. It sounded like a heavy truck stripping its gears. "It has nothing to do with us," she said. "He's a stranger. First time here. Brought his trouble with him."

"You three," Mattei ordered, "go sit on the stairs. Good. Now, Loulou, who else is here?"

"Gizelle's upstairs in bed with the *grippe*. No one else."

"How about Ramon, your faithful husband and partner?"

Loulou paused. Mattei noted her hesitation. "He's out . . . shopping."

Mattei smiled. "He wouldn't be bringing some help and a car, would he? That would make sense. No one wants their front hall cluttered up with a *machabée*, particularly a business establishment like yours."

"He's at Euromart, buying food," Loulou insisted.

Mattei shrugged. "Show me the toilet, Loulou. You girls sit right where you are."

Loulou led him down a dark corridor, past some leggy potted geraniums, to the toilet. The door hung from its hinges, shattered into splinters. The cream-colored wall was splattered with blood, and the footrests of the stand-up toilet were awash with it.

Mattei grimaced and sniffed at the strong odor of gunpowder. He ran his finger over what was left of the door, picking up a smudge from deep powder burns.

"I would say a 'widow-maker,' " he commented, "a double-barreled, sawed-off widow-maker with heavy boar shot. Wouldn't you?"

Loulou tossed her cigarette butt into the blood-filled toilet and lit another. "I wouldn't know. It's not my business."

"Oh?" Mattei cautioned, "I wouldn't count on that, Loulou."

He heard a car pull up as they walked to the back hall. He drew his Colt and motioned for them all to be quiet. Ramon rushed through the open door. He stopped abruptly when he saw Mattei.

"Come in, come in," Mattei said, moving toward the door and pushing Ramon against the wall. He glanced out at the Peugeot sedan Ramon had left with its motor running, and gave Loulou's husband a thorough frisking.

"Now sit on the stairs like a good boy," Mattei told him. "How many were they?" he asked, turning to Loulou again.

"Two," she replied. "They were here before he came. They took a room."

Mattei looked at the prostitutes sitting like faded schoolgirls on the stairs. "Who was with them?"

"Nobody," Loulou said. "They ordered a bottle of champagne and said they'd pick someone later."

"And this one?" Mattei asked, nodding toward the corpse.

"He took Marina," Loulou said, indicating the overweight brunette with plucked eyebrows.

"Well?" Mattei asked, waiting for Marina to talk.

"He said little," Marina told him. "He was with me only a short time. Pam, pam, and it was over. He left and then the explosion downstairs."

Mattei crouched beside the body to reach inside the man's jacket. He brought his hand out empty and wiped it free of blood on the jacket's sleeve.

"Go get his wallet," he said flatly.

Marina began to protest, but Loulou cut her short. "Do what he says," she ordered.

As Marina climbed the stairs, a small patrol car pulled up outside and three uniformed policemen got out. "Bonjour, Chef," Mattei greeted the ranking officer. "Took your time getting here."

"Sorry, Inspecteur, the traffic was heavy and they'd told us not to use our klaxon."

"Never mind," Mattei sighed. "Look, I can't stay around. Get an ambulance for the quiet one and bring this crowd in. Keep them apart until you take their statements. The bad boys had a room upstairs. Seal it and call in the technicians."

Marina returned and handed Mattei a lizard-skin wallet. He went through it quickly, noting a picture of the dead man with a wife and two small children, several thousand in franc notes, and a professional card labeling its bearer as a building contractor with an office address in Nice.

"Aha!" Mattei commented. *Les Niçois* were persistent. Mattei guessed the dead contractor was another casualty in the long struggle between the Nice gangs and the old families of the Marseille underworld. "See that this wallet and everything in it gets to Carso in Antigang," he told the policeman. "Tell him I'll be in touch later."

"Inspecteur!?" A policeman called from the car. "Radio for you."

Mattei lumbered over to the car and took the mouthpiece, pressing the button. "Mattei here."

"*Alors?*" Bastide's voice sputtered, "what the hell are you doing in Endoume?"

"Some pros gunned down a contractor from Nice. Lenoir wasn't available, so . . ."

"He's on his way," Bastide said. "I need you on the Feldman case. Your check on Costin's in. It's hot."

"On my way." Mattei clipped the mouthpiece back on the radio and motioned for the senior policeman to join him outside the hotel.

"I'm leaving," Mattei told him. "Keep your eye on all of them. Search Marina's room. I'm sure she helped herself to a bonus from that wallet. After all, he was a family man."

The Feldmans had invited Hank Castel to lunch at their hotel. He'd managed to find a wrinkled necktie among the jumble of his clothing and he looked fairly presentable. Without her dark glasses, Mrs. Feldman looked surprisingly like Ginnie. Mr. Feldman had obviously impressed the hotel's staff. The maître d'hôtel and the waiters responded quickly and efficiently to his requests. The hotel dining room was a throwback to prewar France. The ceilings were high, the leather banquettes were trimmed with metal rods, and large vases of pink stock decorated the wide serving tables. Conversation remained at a low pitch; only the sound of a cork being pulled or the clink of silverware disturbed the calm.

Castel finished his duck-liver pâté and drank some wine.

"How do you like it?" Mr. Feldman asked.

"It's good."

"Comes from here. I always believe in drinking the local wines when I'm traveling. Old stuffed shirt over there," he indicated the maître d'hôtel, "always recommends an expensive Bordeaux. Last night, he reminded me that champagne goes with everything."

Mrs. Feldman put down her fork and a waiter appeared to clear the remnants of the first course from the table. Castel was still ill at ease. Ginnie's name had not been mentioned. Her father seemed to be making a special effort to appear relaxed and pleasant. Even her mother had participated in the conversation. The waiters reappeared to serve them from covered silver dishes. Mr. Feldman ordered another bottle of wine.

"Eat," Mrs. Feldman urged, indicating Castel's plate of fricassee chicken with morel mushrooms. "It'll get cold."

"Hank," Mr. Feldman said, slicing into his lamb, "we're leaving tomorrow."

"Oh?"

"Yes, we're taking Ginnie home. It will be a big funeral. We've got a lot of family."

Mrs. Feldman was toying with her oversized omelet. "Is Beckie Roth coming?" she asked her husband.

"I don't know," he replied. "She's out in L.A. If she can, she will."

Mr. Feldman frowned, obviously resenting his wife's interjection. "Listen, Hank," he said, "you're the only person here I can trust. The Willington crowd seem to be a nest of losers, and that Craig . . . I just don't like. Miss Chappel means well, I guess, but she's obviously a lush. We'll be coming back, at least I will. But, while we're gone we'd like to feel there was someone representing us. You see my point?"

Hank was surprised, caught off balance, and slightly angry. He was being roped in again. He resented Feldman's obvious assurance and his gratuitous comments on Willington.

"I don't think you're being fair to everyone at Willington," he said, "particularly to Marcia Chappel. She was very upset at your daughter's death."

"We know, dear," Mrs. Feldman said. "Fred didn't mean to be so hard. He's still nervous."

"I didn't mean to insult anyone, Hank," Feldman explained, pausing to sip from his glass. "I just would like you to help us."

"But what can I do? I'm not a detective," Castel said. "I'm not an informer, either."

"Hey, hold it," Feldman said laughingly. "If I wanted a spy I'd dial the CIA. No, look, you've got it wrong. I'd like someone to keep in touch with the police, follow the case. Someone to call me . . . every day if necessary. I want to stay on top of this, even from a distance."

"Look, Mr. Feldman," Hank Castel replied, "I'm a student. I've got a lot of work to do. I've got exams. I'd like them to find Ginnie's murderer too, but I can't make it a full-time occupation."

Feldman filled his mouth with lamb and scalloped potatoes. He chewed slowly, eyeing Castel. When he'd swallowed and downed some more wine, he leaned across the table toward him.

"I'd be paying you, of course," he said. "You name your price."

Hank Castel put his napkin down on the table. His face was flushed, his mouth a straight line. "Thanks for dinner," he murmured. "Excuse me. I've got to go. Good night."

Mr. Feldman watched in astonishment as Castel left the dining room. "What the hell is his problem?" he asked his wife.

"His problem is he's a nice boy and you've insulted him," Mrs. Feldman explained. "Freddie, sometimes you're just stupid about people."

Feldman shrugged. "I don't get it. We have a nice dinner. He was a friend of Ginnie's. I ask a little favor and he walks out."

Mrs. Feldman took her first sip of wine.

Feldman half rose in his seat, peering toward the door, hoping that Castel might have changed his mind. "He's too damn sensitive," he murmured, sitting down again.

"That," Mrs. Feldman remarked, "you should try."

Mattei finished reading the telexed report on Professor Costin and handed it back to Bastide. "I would say we've got a prime suspect."

Bastide walked to his desk and leaned against it, thinking. "It looks that way," he finally replied, putting the telex down, "but seducing a female student in Toul doesn't make him a murderer or a pervert."

Mattei took off his blazer and slung it over the back of his chair. "So," he speculated, "the professor sees the Feldman girl in his class, he yearns to relive what happened at Toul, he makes his move and the little American says, 'Non, merci.' Costin is furious, insulted, touched to the quick. He waits for her at her apartment and, *toc, toc, toc,* within seconds she looks like a pincushion."

Bastide sat behind his desk. "A good scenario, Babar, but too easy, too simple."

"We deserve something easy and simple for a change," Mattei commented.

"Don't count on it," Bastide warned. "I talked to the DST. It seems Costin has a highly political past. Red flag, black flag and, before Willington, a couple of years teaching in Algeria's revolutionary paradise. So, you see, this one won't be easy or simple."

"I liked him better," Mattei sighed, "when it was just young girls."

Bastide glanced at his watch. "Let's have lunch at Chez Étienne before we return to Aix."

"Agree. I'm starved. Don't you think we'd be smart to rent a damn room in Aix? I hate commuting."

They parked the unmarked police sedan just off the rue de la République and climbed the ancient stone stairway that led into the Panier district, a warren of narrow, cobbled streets and alleys overlooking the Vieux Port and the harbor. Chez Étienne, on the rue de Lorette, was popular with the police, the press and the more adventurous businessmen of Marseille. Its small, shabby façade promised little, but once inside, the tempting odors of oven-browned pizza and grilled meat explained the daily crush of customers.

Shortly after pushing open the door, Bastide and Mattei were standing at the far end of the narrow dining room drinking a glass of the house red wine and waiting to be seated. The old brick pizza oven glowed with heat, the two waitresses swiveled through the narrow aisles laden with dishes, bottles and wineglasses. Étienne, a thin man with a wry, knowing smile moved from table to table, seeing to the needs of his customers. The restaurant was noisy, full of loud talk and laughter. A well-rounded blond waitress squeezed past Mattei on her way to the kitchen. He smiled broadly at Bastide.

"That one is all real," he joked.

"So is her husband . . . a very big truck driver."

Étienne gestured to them, indicating two empty chairs at a nearby table. "That's it," Étienne said as they sat down. "Keep your glasses and I'll bring a bottle." He handed them the menus and hurried off.

"I'm having a pizza," Mattei said, "with anchovies."

"I'm for tiny squid," Bastide remarked. "He marinates them and gives them a quick grilling. I've tried it at home, but I can't get the same flavor."

Étienne returned with a bottle and they ordered.

"So . . . it's back to Aix," Mattei said. "You don't have to come, you know. I can handle the professor."

"No, I want another look at him. Particularly while you're asking the questions. I forgot to tell you, the girl's parents are taking her home tomorrow. Mr. Feldman called me. He knows a few words of French and I managed a few of English. He's leaving his American telephone number at Willington and he wants us to call him collect if we have any news. He said he'd probably be coming back."

"That's not good," Mattei commented. "He'll only get in the way, nosing around. Talking about nosing around . . . have you seen Aynard today?"

"No. But his secretary called. He wants me to check in every evening with a 'progress report.' "

Their waitress arrived with the pizza and squid. She warned them about the hot plates and left a small basket of sliced baguette on the table. The tiny squid were still sizzling and redolent of garlic. The pizza was golden brown and bubbling, fresh from the oven. Bastide broke a piece of bread and dipped it into the highly spiced squid sauce.

"Moments like this," he said, smiling and chewing, "make living in Marseille worthwhile."

"Despite Aynard," Mattei added, filling their wineglasses.

CHAPTER IV

Dr. Gregg had insisted on giving a traditional Thanksgiving luncheon for a few French guests and some carefully selected students. Gregg was eager to disassociate Willington with what had happened to Ginne Feldman, to make people think of other things. Marcia Chappel had made a special effort with the table, and some of the faculty wives had been dragooned into contributing a special dish or some pastry to the meal. A contact at the American consulate in Marseille had managed to procure a huge, prebasted Butterball turkey from a U.S. Navy ship. It was now browning and sputtering in the oven, watched apprehensively by the Greggs' Spanish cook, who'd never seen such an enormous fowl in her life.

The candle-lit table was decorated with a centerpiece of three pumpkins in a large bowl. Two small American flags marked the occasion as a national holiday. Cut-crystal serving dishes offered celery and olives, roasted nuts and cheese straws. There were two mince pies, a huge, deep pumpkin pie and a chocolate layer cake on the nearby sideboard.

Marcia Chappel had spread an assortment of fall leaves along the table, hoping to achieve the effect she'd accomplished in New England, but the French leaves wouldn't cooperate. They weren't gold-tipped or scarlet from the frost . . . just dark and dead from the Provençal dampness. Luckily a longtime American resident of Aix had loaned her some small place-card holders in the form of turkeys to add to the ambiance.

Madame de Rozier was one of the first to be seated. She maintained a thin smile, surveying the table without enthusiasm and toying with her amber beads. She considered the yearly Thanksgiving invitations a form of ordeal. Each American university group usually had some form of celebration, and she was invited to all of them. It wasn't that she disliked the holiday itself; it was the menu she detested. She knew little about American history, but she was sure that if the Indians had eaten corn and sweet yams it was out of necessity and not choice. She couldn't understand why her American friends insisted on subjecting their French colleagues to such culinary torture.

She watched the other guests from her place of honor to the right of the host. She noted the mayor and the sous-préfet had sent assistants to take their places . . . no yams and corn for them. There were some male and female students at both ends of the table. She recognized Hank Castel. At least he spoke understandable French. A visiting American professor from California took the seat to her right. He was a heavy man with a well-trimmed beard, a political scientist working on a study of the Third Republic. His French was technically correct but full of painful stops and starts. She'd talked to him briefly over drinks before luncheon. He told her how pleased he was to be placed at her side. She treated him to a full-three-second smile. The American professor's wife was across the table from Madame de Rozier. She was a rawboned woman with tinted auburn hair. She defiantly placed a pack of cigarettes and a lighter on the table as if challenging someone to protest. Madame de Rozier watched Marcia Chappel sipping the drink she'd carried to the table from the other room. The ridges of a frown creased Madame de Rozier's heavily powdered forehead. That woman's liver, she thought, must be hard as a rock.

"Friends," Dr. Gregg intoned, standing and smiling down at all of them, "welcome to our Thanksgiving table. Before we make a brief offering of thanks, let me say a few words about the origins of this day." Gregg then launched into a homily about the Pilgrim Fathers, the *Mayflower*, the landing at Plymouth Rock and the first Thanksgiving. The American professor's wife sighed audibly and stifled a yawn.

Madame de Rozier's thoughts were far from the windswept shores of Massachusetts. Her mind was on the Feldman case. The police were much too slow. She hadn't heard of any progress, and she had a suspicion that Commissaire Aynard was avoiding her calls. How things had changed! The Socialists were making a mess of everything. Now even the police were undependable. She remembered the words of her late husband, the Count de Rozier, shortly before his death.

"They aren't bad people," he'd told her, "they're just little people."

As far as she was concerned, he had been too optimistic. She decided to ring Commissaire Aynard again after the luncheon. A flurry of discreet applause followed Dr. Gregg's speech. He sat down, folded his hands and bowed his head. The others followed suit as he offered thanks.

The first course, a thin consommé with a floating slice of lemon, was served by the cook's daughter. There was a murmur of conversation as spoons were lifted, and Dr. Gregg put his hand on hers in a friendly gesture.

"I hope you like our lunch," he said.

"I'm sure I will," she lied. "I always love celebrating Thanksgiving."

The cook's son appeared in a tight black suit to pour the dry sherry. Madame de Rozier tasted her consommé, noted it had come from a tin and recalled that she still had to face the turkey, with its strangely flavored stuffing and cloying cranberry sauce, the candied yams, the tinned corn, the creamed onions, the turnips and the heavy, mashed potatoes. Worst of all, she dreaded the pumpkin pie. She would never understand why someone would want to make a pie from the soggy scrapings of a *citrouille.*

Jean Bates had to put her face within inches of the mirror to apply her mascara and eye shadow. She proceeded methodically, blinking and pausing to tilt her head, gauging the effect of her efforts. She'd fluffed her hair into a blond halo and put on some gold loop earrings. Her heavy, young breasts were straining at the sheer material of her newly purchased French bra. The matching panties were much too tight, cutting into the soft flesh of her upper thighs.

She was happy and looking forward to the day. Normally, she'd still be in bed, covered with blankets, dreading the thought of getting up. Half the time, she'd be coming off a high or fighting a hangover, and the thought of spending a few hours in the Willington classrooms was enough to make her physically ill. Jean

Bates was the type of young woman who didn't ask herself personal questions, but she was smart enough to know that she'd undergone some sort of change. It had all begun with the minstrel. He fascinated her. Thinking about him sent a delicious thrill through her body. She'd seen him three times since their first meeting. They got along well together. She found him handsome and appealing. She'd never had the same feeling for a man before. He'd suggested she stop popping pills or smoking pot for a few days, and she'd done it.

She finished her eyes and sighed, putting away her brushes and bottles. She wondered if she was in love. How could she be sure? She might know by the end of the day. He'd invited her out to his cabin at Le Tholonet. It would be the first time they'd be alone, and she couldn't wait. Just the thought of making love to the minstrel excited her. She stepped back from the mirror, examining herself. They'd called her pudgy when she'd been in grammar school, and someone at Willington had once jokingly labeled her "our Miss Piggy." She couldn't see the justification for such comments. She considered herself voluptuous. Men liked that. She knew from experience. She turned, examining her profile, lifted her breasts, sucking in her stomach.

"Not bad," she said to herself and walked over to the gas heater, holding out her hands for some warmth. She wanted to look just right. Everything had to be perfect.

Bastide pressed the doorbell of the small rooming house off the Place des Tanneurs. He could hear it reverberating from the walls inside. The woman who opened the heavy door was short, gray-haired and suspicious. She wiped her hands on a stained blue apron and pulled the door toward her while she waited for Bastide to speak.

"Well?" she queried, looking past Bastide to Mattei, obviously disapproving of both of them.

"Professor Pierre Costin," Bastide replied, "is he here?"

"He's left."

"Left?"

"That's what I said. Listen, young man, I have a washing to do . . ."

Bastide flicked open his wallet and put his police identity card under her nose. "Police Judiciaire," he told her. "Inspecteurs Bastide and Mattei."

The woman was unimpressed. "So?"

"Listen, little mother," Mattei cut in threateningly, moving forward.

"*Doucement,*" Bastide warned, blocking him. He pocketed his wallet and smiled. "Madame, we need your help. When did the professor leave? Where was he going and when is he coming back?"

She rose on her toes to get a better look at Mattei, frowned at him and replied. "He left early this morning. I don't know where he went. I don't pry into the affairs of my roomers. He told me nothing of his return."

"Thank you," Bastide said, unconvinced. "We'd like a look at his room."

"I don't know—"

It was Bastide's turn to be irritated with her intransigence. "I suggest you cooperate," he snapped, his voice hard. "Now, show us to his room."

His sudden brusqueness impressed her. She grudgingly pulled the door wider and let them in, while pointing at the mat on the tile floor. When they'd wiped their shoes, she led them upstairs to the first floor and unlocked a door halfway down the hall. The room was bare and painted a bilious green. There was a minimum of furniture or decoration. A small writing table faced the window, which looked out onto a blank wall. The old brass bed was narrow and sagging. A chest of drawers was pushed against one wall, and a small washbasin was half hidden behind a screen of cheap flowered material. There were a number of books on the chest, propped between two art-nouveau bookends, and a pile of magazines in a corner. Bastide opened the drawers one by one. They held underwear and shirts. Mattei looked under the bed. Nothing but dust and some old cigarette butts.

"Does he owe you money?" Bastide demanded.

"No," she replied, "he paid me yesterday for the whole month."

"Tell us about Professor Costin," Bastide said, walking to the window and peering behind the curtains.

The landlady shrugged. "He is quiet. Pleasant enough. He reads a lot."

"Did he have any women friends? Ever bring them here?"

"No."

"Well, go on."

"He spends a lot of time correcting papers. He takes his meals at L'Arcade, the restaurant on the Place de l'Hôtel de Ville. I don't think he likes his work."

"Why do you say that?"

"Oh, he always comes home in a black mood. I can tell. I kidded him once or twice about his *amerloque* students. He didn't think it was funny, so I stopped. We have little to say to each other."

Mattei had finished looking under the pillows. He squatted down to inspect the magazines. There were several back issues of *Le Nouvelle Observateur*, two copies of the Sunday *L'Humanité* and some publications he didn't recognize. He leafed through them quickly, identifying them as left-wing journals, from the predominance of revolutionary prose, photos of CGT demonstrations and anti-American cartoons. There was a manila envelope on the bottom of the pile. He opened it and shook out some photos.

"Oho!" he murmured, turning his back to the landlady. "Roger, come here a minute."

Bastide interrupted his questioning and joined Mattei.

"What do you think?" Mattei asked, shuffling through the photos one at a time.

Each photo depicted a young girl in a lewd or erotic pose. Some were nude, others wore garter belts and black net hose, others were feigning ecstasy. A set of photos brought two girls together.

Mattei smiled, turning to Bastide. "Our professor obviously has a problem."

Bastide turned a photo and read the descriptive paragraph stamped on its back. "Yvonne and Marie wait till their husbands go to work to have some fun. Wouldn't you like to join in? Further exclusive scenes of their pleasures are available at bargain prices. Write to Amourama, 739 rue Thourin, Paris X^e, for our catalogue, enclosing 50 francs to cover mailing costs."

The landlady edged forward, curious, but Bastide took the

photos from Mattei, stuffed them back in the envelope and put it
under his arm.

"What's the professor done?" she asked.

"Nothing at all," Bastide told her. "But we'd like to talk to him.
He didn't leave an address or telephone number?"

"No. But he'll be back," she told them.

"How do you know that?"

She seemed surprised at the question. "He is employed in Aix."

Bastide was suddenly tired of the pointless conversation. "Give
Madame our coordinates," he said to Mattei over his shoulder.
"I'm going to get some fresh air."

The narrow strip of light blue sky showing above the street was
spotted with silky white clouds. Bastide turned up the collar of his
trench coat and pulled out the leather cigar case Janine had given
him for his forty-first birthday. He selected one of the stubby
Upmanns, pierced its end with a small penknife and struck a
match. He puffed at the cigar gently, savoring its rich flavor, and
leaned against the wall to wait for Mattei.

He wasn't quite sure what to make of Costin's absence. Was he
really on the run? He'd paid a month's rent, but that could have
been an amateurish attempt to cover his tracks. All the evidence
was pointing to the professor. With such continued luck, they
might be able to wrap things up quickly and give Aynard what he
wanted: a nice, uncomplicated solution. And yet . . . something
bothered Bastide. If Costin was obsessed with sex, why hadn't the
girl been sexually violated? Why were there no traces of violence
in Costin's past?

Bastide watched an old man shuffling along the sidewalk on his
way to the bakery across the street. He carried a sagging string bag
full of vegetables, and his left hand was twitching with palsy. Bastide thought of his father. He'd been dead for eleven years, but
every time Bastide passed the fishing port of Le Vallon-des-Auffes
he felt the sharp pain of real loss. His father had been a fisherman
in the best tradition of Marseille. A hardy, exuberant man attuned
to the sea and tempered by the winds. Antoine Bastide had been a
true professional. His small fishing boat, *Le Rascasse*, had always
been where the fish were, in the cold, windswept early morning or
bobbing off the Corniche on balmy nights when the squid rose like

undulating ghosts toward their light. A *bon vivant* and *gros mangeur*, Antoine Bastide had been gentle and caring with his wife and children. Then the sea he'd known so well had tricked him. One of those sudden, treacherous storms, a passing dark smudge on the horizon, had caught him and young Caillou unexpectedly. They'd found Caillou clinging to the overturned boat hours later. It had taken forty-eight hours to find his father's body.

"Voilà," Mattei commented, pulling on his cap. "I left the old bitch recounting her money. She wanted to make sure Costin hadn't pulled a fast one. You ready to go?"

Bastide stopped daydreaming. "Yes," he replied, the Havana between his teeth. "We'd better get over to Willington. I want to see if Dr. Gregg knows about Costin's departure."

The rocky mass of Mont Sainte Victoire was distinct and dominating in the sunlight. It rose over the countryside near Tholonet like a giant, irregular wall, the early-afternoon shadows accentuating the cuts and ravines in its stone face. The uneven valley was dotted with shuttered summer villas and small farmhouses with thin wisps of smoke rising from their chimneys. Groves of twisted olive trees marched to the sandy base of the mountain, and stands of cypress swayed in the wind near the winding *route départemental*.

The minstrel filled Jean Bates's glass with more *eau de vie*. It was cheap and raw, but he couldn't afford anything better. Jean Bates was talkative and gay. She'd found the setting romantic. The more she watched the minstrel move around the small cabin, the more sexually attractive he became. Her nearsighted brown eyes were soft and vulnerable as she lifted her glass.

"To you," she said huskily, trying her best to sound like Marilyn Monroe.

"To you, Jean," he replied, draining his *eau de vie* with a quick tilt of his head.

"Come sit next to me," she purred, patting the rough bench. He smiled, refilled his glass and moved to her side. He was wearing tight, faded jeans and a torn gray turtleneck sweater. A headband kept his long hair out of his eyes and off his pale forehead.

"Do you like this dump?" he asked, gesturing at the thick, whitewashed walls, the wrought-iron utensils near the open fireplace and the pots and jars filled with dried wildflowers on the window-sill.

"I love it," she murmured, putting her hand on his thigh and gazing out the small window to the old stone fence and the tall rocks at the base of Montagne Sainte Victoire. This was what France was all about, as far as she was concerned. Not the dull classes and the stupid exams. This was romance with a capital R. Just like the flicks . . . only better. She'd take the minstrel any day over Robert Redford.

He was looking down at the back of her neck, examining her meticulously with his thin mouth pursed. He seemed deep in thought. Her hand moved slowly to the tight crotch of his jeans. He winced, pulling away slightly, and she turned toward him, surprised.

"Hey, kid," he said jokingly, his slight German accent making the archaic slang seem even more dated, "let's go for a walk before we get serious."

She was disappointed, but ready to do anything he suggested. "Okay," she said, "but where's the john?"

"It's out in back. Just behind the kitchen."

She laughed. "Out in back? You really are roughing it."

She stood up, tucking her blouse into her pants, turning to give him a good look at the swell of her breasts under the sheer material. He watched her go out the door, folded his arms and began to whistle a lilting tune he remembered from his childhood. Everything had been fine until his mother had married the *ami*, the American sergeant with the idiot grin and the small sports car. As he grew older, she'd told him how lucky she'd been to find a husband, to find him a father. She'd never told him who his real father had been. She still hadn't. He knew why. She didn't know. His face turned ugly as he thought about Sergeant John Warren. Warren had called Otto "buddy" and insisted on putting his arms around his shoulders in front of guests. Otto had been on his own since Warren had retired and taken Otto's mother to live in Virginia.

Jean Bates bounced back into the room. "Ready to go?" she asked.

"Yes," he told her. "Come on, I want to show you the caves I've found at the base of the mountain."

"That sounds like fun."

She put on her down jacket and zipped it tightly.

"Can you live on what you make singing in the street?" she asked as they went out the door.

"No, I've got a job."

"Where?"

"Down in Marseille. Three days a week."

"Doing what?"

"Tossing ice around."

Dr. Gregg was distant and abrupt when Bastide and Mattei called at his residence. He explained that he still had luncheon guests. Bastide could hear the murmur of conversation through the half-open door leading into the sitting room. Gregg knew nothing of Costin's whereabouts. He pointed out that all professors and students had the day off, as it was an American holiday. He suggested that Costin may have made plans to turn his day off into a long weekend.

"Why do you want to see Professor Costin?" Dr. Gregg asked, his suspicions aroused.

"We had a few more questions for him," Bastide explained.

Marcia Chappel appeared at the door. "Oh," she said, surprised to see the police. "I'm sorry," she told Gregg, "but Madame de Rozier has consented to play the piano for us."

"You'll have to excuse me," Gregg said, nodding to Bastide and Mattei and going back to his guests. Marcia Chappel hesitated.

"Can I be of help?" she asked.

"We're trying to locate Professor Costin," Bastide told her. "Do you have any idea where he might go for a long weekend?"

She thought for a few seconds before replying. "He sometimes goes off for a cure. Like many Frenchmen, he—" She stopped, embarrassed.

"He is worried about his liver?" Bastide volunteered.

She laughed. "Exactly. He believes in a periodic 'cleansing.'"

"Do you know where he goes?"

"Yes, he once mentioned the Clinique de Vaucluse, near Carpentras."

Mattei scribbled the notation as Bastide said good-bye and made excuses for the interruption.

"But why Professor Costin?" Marcia Chappel asked. "Is there a problem?"

"No, no," Bastide said, "just routine questions. We like to know where everyone is. Au revoir, mademoiselle."

"*Eh ba, merde!*" Mattei growled as they walked away from the Willington house. "Our murderer, our satyr on the run, turns into a nervous cholesterol watcher in love with his own liver."

"We don't know that yet," Bastide cautioned. "Let's get down to Guignon's office and call that clinic. If he isn't there, we'll have our work cut out for us."

By the time they got back to Marseille, the sky was low and loosing its first heavy drops on the traffic-clogged streets. They had reached Professor Costin from Aix. He had come to the telephone hesitantly, surprised at being called away from his grated-carrot salad and mineral water. He had obviously been nervous. He told Bastide he planned to return on Monday in time for his afternoon class. He'd wanted to know what had prompted their call. Bastide reminded Costin that he'd asked the staff and students at Willington to stay in the Aix region or notify him if anyone had to travel. Bastide had wished him luck with his cure and rung off.

He decided to eat at Le Haiphong. He hadn't seen Dinh Le Thong for a few weeks. Thong was a former Vietnamese parachutist, a *baroudeur* whom Bastide had served with in Algeria. He was a stocky, powerful man with spiky gray hair, high cheekbones and the eyes of a Mongol warrior. He'd been recruited into the French Government's undercover action section, *les barbouzes*, to use counterterrorist tactics against the OAS, the Secret Army Organization trying to topple the DeGaulle government. Half of his left hand was missing, thanks to the premature explosion of a charge he was setting in the basement of an OAS villa near Tipasa.

Le Haiphong was a clearinghouse for information on what was happening or about to happen among the many Asian residents of Marseille. In addition to his countrymen, Thong had contacts with the Cambodians, the Laotians and the Meo, Man, Thai, Nung and Thô tribal refugees scattered throughout the Bouches du Rhône Département. Le Haiphong was also a very good restaurant, specializing in the cuisine of North Vietnam.

Bastide pushed open the red-lacquered door of Le Haiphong and entered a replica of a back-street restaurant in that port city. The piquant odor of *nuoc-mâm* and coriander dominated the dining room. A Vietnamese song with a strange tonality was playing in the background, the female voice changing register constantly. The tables were covered with white, disposable paper and set with paper napkins, chopsticks, small vials of soy sauce and nuoc-mâm and a jar of crushed peppers in oil. A cheap glass vase on each table held a yellow plastic rose. The walls were red, and a gold trim of rustic dragons ran the length of the room. There were paintings of North Vietnam, the Baie d'Along, the upper reaches of the Red River and the mountains near Laichau behind the bar at the far end of the room.

Dinh Le Thong left his abacus on the bar and advanced to shake hands with Bastide. *"Bonjour, Chef,"* he greeted the inspector. "You'll eat, surely?"

"Yes, *vieux*. That's why I'm here."

Thong led Bastide to the last table in the restaurant. "Voilà," Thong said, "you can watch the door from here and I'll watch the rear. Just like old times."

Bastide reached across the table and poked Thong affectionately on the shoulder with his fist. "I don't have to watch my front and rear any more," Bastide commented.

Thong looked doubtful. He shook his head. *"Mon cher,* never relax. I don't even now. That's why I'm still alive."

Bastide saw that Thong was serious. He liked the aging warrior. They'd been in some tight spots together during the battle for Algiers. They'd been involved in the undercover war against the FLN in the small alleys and back streets. No quarter asked or given. Bastide remembered the horror, the assassinations, the torture, the mutilations, the bombings. Thong had moved through it all with serenity, tracking, ambushing, killing with a professional coolness that had shocked the young Bastide. But Thong had been born to war and violence. By the time he left North Vietnam for

Algeria, in 1954, he already held the Croix de Guerre with two palms, and the Médaille Militaire. His body bore scars from innumerable skirmishes and battles in the Tonkin Delta and the mountain country near the Chinese border.

A young waitress in a traditional *ao dai* moved gracefully toward them and handed Bastide a menu.

"No, no," Thong said, snatching the menu from Bastide's hand and sending the waitress away. "I'll order your dinner. I know what is good tonight. Are you hungry?"

Bastide hadn't thought much about food, but the atmosphere and the enticing odors from the kitchen were sharpening his appetite.

"Yes, I could do justice to a good meal."

Thong nodded, satisfied. He stood up, reached across the bar and put a bottle of Johnnie Walker black label between them. He handed a glass to Bastide and took one himself. When he'd poured each of them a three-finger measure, he lifted his glass. Bastide would have preferred wine, but the whiskey was part of an established ritual.

"To our dead."

"To our dead," Bastide repeated. It was a simple, somber toast.

Thong left Bastide to drink his whiskey and ducked into the kitchen. Four other tables were occupied. A Vietnamese family were gathered around the large central table, the mother serving the raven-haired children from a large bowl while the father sucked noisily at his soup and a grey-haired grandmother fed the youngest child with her chopsticks. Two of the other tables were taken by French couples. There were three Asian men at the fourth table. Bastide couldn't see them too well. They were half hidden by a large oriental urn. He leaned a bit to his left for a better look. One of the men raised his eyes at the same time, smiled and nodded. Bastide nodded abruptly, embarrassed.

"Who the hell is that type?" he asked Thong when he turned.

"You don't recognize him? It's Ngoan . . . of the DST. You met him here last year around Christmas."

Bastide recalled the chubby, well-mannered DST agent who was assigned to keep his eye on all newly arrived Asian refugees.

"*Bon sang!*" Bastide remarked, "he's getting fat as a pig."

"So would you," Thong laughed, "if you spent your day eating in every oriental restaurant south of Valence."

The waitress put a steaming bowl of soup on the table. The beef bouillon and rice noodles were topped by thin strips of beef that had been cooked by the boiling bouillon. Chopped chervil, onion, tarragon, chives and a few coriander leaves had been sprinkled over the meat.

"*Pho tai!*" Thong announced proudly. "A simple dish, but one that will give you strength. The perfect antidote to this weather. Here, have some nuoc-mâm."

Bastide helped himself to the shallow dish of the fish sauce, squeezed a quarter of a lemon over it and added some of the oily hot pepper. He mixed it together with his chopsticks and poured a small amount into his soup. He took a mouthful of broth, beef and noodles.

"You like it?" Thong asked.

Bastide indicated Thong should be patient, that he couldn't reply with his mouth full. "*Formidable!*" he finally replied.

Thong's weathered face lit up at the praise. He was as much a cook as he had been a professional soldier.

"What are you working on?" Thong asked as Bastide continued eating his soup.

"A murder at Aix. A girl . . . an American student."

"How?" Thong was always interested in weapons and methods.

"Probably an ice pick. Small puncture wounds, a lot of them."

Thong toyed with a chopstick. He smiled. "You know, this is one of the best killing tools," he mused, tapping the chopstick on the edge of Bastide's bowl. "All the pressure of a well-aimed thrust concentrated on that tiny, rounded point of rock-hard bamboo. You only have to know where to place it." He sighed and put the chopstick down. "Do you have a suspect?"

Bastide grunted ruefully. "We did, up to a few hours ago. Now I'm not sure."

"This girl was young?"

"Yes."

"A shame. I hate the murderers of women. It's as if they've stamped on a flower. I'll ask my people in Aix to keep their ears open. Who knows, they might be able to help."

Bastide finished his soup. "That would be useful," he told Thong. "We need all the help we can get."

Thong made a clicking noise with his tongue, catching the waitress's attention. She came to clear away the soup bowl and smiled shyly at Bastide. Thong noticed Bastide's sudden interest.

"Holà," he warned, "that is my niece. She's only sixteen and she is a good waitress. Careful, or I'll tell Mademoiselle Janine."

"Ça va," Bastide replied, changing the subject. "What is the next dish?"

"Duck with lotus buds. My ancestors used it as an aphrodisiac. Do you think you can handle it tonight?"

"Just keep your so-called niece out of sight, you liar, or I'll introduce her to *your* wife."

Professor Costin would have no trouble eating lightly at dinner. Bastide's telephone call had upset him. He had planned to reread some Sartre over his meal, but he couldn't concentrate. He surveyed the dining room of the Clinique de Vaucluse while he waited to be served. The aged couple from Poitiers were picking at their plate of raw vegetables and cutting their grilled sole into tiny pieces to make it last. They looked like two drowsy turtles perched on the edge of a pond. Costin knew that in a few minutes they would finish, rise unsteadily and begin a slow, nerve-wracking traverse of the dining room that seemed to last forever. They'd done it at lunch. He fully expected them to crash to the floor totally incapacitated by their efforts.

His cheerful, chubby waiter brought him a plate of gray boiled beef and steamed turnips. He set it down with a flourish, poured more Vittel water into Costin's glass and pirouetted over to the elderly couple to ask how they were doing. Costin looked away to spare himself the sight of loose dentures bared in grateful smiles.

He had left Aix not only for his health. He'd wanted to spend some time thinking. It had become very important to him. In his haste, he'd forgotten that he was not to leave the city. What a fool! Now the police must be suspicious. If they started digging into his past . . . if they found out about Toul . . . He sliced a piece of beef and speared it with his fork. He felt that it was time to make a decision. If he returned to Aix, the police were sure to question him again. He put the meat into his mouth and chewed. It had the consistency of uncured leather.

He dabbed at his mouth with a napkin, trying to concentrate. He did not kill the Feldman girl. At least that was a starting point. But was it? It really made no difference as far as he was concerned. It wasn't the murder that bothered him. It was the effect of the murder on his future. If Dr. Gregg heard of the incident in Toul, he'd be finished . . . out on the street again. He looked up, trying to locate the butter for his turnips, and then realized none would be served. He sipped at his water, trying to force his mind to react as it should, logically and efficiently. He thought of all the philosophers and great thinkers he'd read. He remembered trying to explain their ideas and aspirations to his classes through the study of the French language. Now, when he wanted his own mind to react, it was dormant and dull, like the worst of his students.

He must make a decision. Should he go back to Aix or should he not go back to Aix? If he did go back, he must speak to the police immediately. Bring up Toul himself, before they do. If he did not return, he must decide where to go. It would have to be another country, another job, a new life. He didn't have much money, but he could draw enough from a regional office of his Marseille bank before anyone knew of his plans. He grimaced, remembering that he'd just paid his landlady a month's rent in advance. Then he reprimanded himself for clouding a momentous decision with such minor details.

He felt a certain panic as the decision hung in the balance. His thin frame was hunched over the table as if he were seeking privacy in a public place. His bald head shone with perspiration, and he had put aside his knife and fork. The elderly couple were the catalysts. They were rising shakily from their chairs, the waiter hovering over them, doing what he could to assist. As they aimed their canes in his direction, Costin decided he could not sit through their snail-like progress once again. He found himself leaving the table, hurrying toward the dining-room exit. He'd made his decision. He would not go back to Aix. As he turned toward the corridor leading to his room, he remembered that he had an old friend in Brussels.

Hank Castel was one of the first students to arrive for Professor Costin's Monday-afternoon class. The classroom was glacial. He kept his leather jacket on and tightened the scarf around his neck. He was prepared for the examination and he knew he'd do all right. Other students dragged in one at a time. A wall clock with a cracked face ticked loudly behind the podium, and a faded framed etching of Descartes hung near the door. Castel checked his watch against the wall clock. It was ten minutes after three. Professor Costin was late. He glanced over his shoulder looking for Jean Bates. No sign of her. That wasn't unusual; she cut most of her classes. Castel guessed she was flying again, spinning off on another high. What a waste, he thought. She'll be an old woman at thirty . . . if she's still alive.

He tried to concentrate on his notes, marveling again at the intricacies of the French language. It did give him a feeling of accomplishment when he mastered a new set of rules. He didn't much care for Professor Costin, but he had to admit that Costin was a dedicated teacher. He obviously believed in what he was doing and exhibited a strange missionary zeal that was lost on most of his students.

The thought of Costin brought Ginnie's murder to mind. He'd felt a twinge of guilt after speaking to Inspecteur Mattei about her tenuous acquaintance with the professor. He'd suddenly seen himself as an informer and realized how easy it would be to destroy someone's career by rumor or hearsay. He'd reassured himself by reasoning that any piece of information could be vital and such minor revelations would certainly not hurt the innocent.

He'd only known Ginnie Feldman for a few days, but he'd been drawn into the wake of her death like flotsam in the wake of a ferry. Her father had called twice from New York. Mr. Feldman was not used to taking no for an answer. He'd cajoled, flattered and shouted in an attempt to convince Hank Castel he should act as his eyes and ears in Aix. They'd finally reached a compromise. Castel would call Feldman once a week with a report on the investigation or any developments relating to Ginnie's murder.

"Remember," Feldman had told him. "I can be there in hours if you think I'm needed." I wonder, Castel asked himself, what he's trying to prove?

The other students were getting restless. Two had already left, quoting the nebulous regulation that ten minutes tardiness by any professor cancels the class.

A black student from New Jersey, hair in tight Rastafarian worms, tapped him on the shoulder. "Hey, Hank," he asked, "what's goin' down here, man? Where is that skinny shit?"

"You got me," Castel told him.

"Well, that is *just* fine. The one time I study for that mother's class and he's a no-show. That cuts it!"

Hank Castel shrugged, gathered up his books and prepared to leave. It was now twenty-five minutes after three. He felt let down. He'd been all primed for the examination; he knew he'd have done well. Now he'd have to gear up all over again. He decided to ask Marcia Chappel about Costin and find out when the exam would be rescheduled.

Marcia Chappel had just put down the phone as he walked into her office. She looked distracted as he asked about Professor Costin.

"He's not there," she murmured with an air of puzzlement.

"He's not where?" Castel asked.

"At the clinic. He left the clinic on Saturday."

He didn't know what she was talking about. "What clinic?" he asked. "Is he sick?"

"No, he was taking a short cure over the weekend. He was due to return in time for his class today."

"I've just come from the class. Maybe he's been delayed?"

"Since Saturday? It's really disturbing." Marcia Chappel frowned and chewed on her lower lip. "The police were looking for him on Thanksgiving Day," she volunteered. "I wonder . . ."

"Wonder what?"

"The police. Perhaps I should call them?"

Hank Castel shook his head. "Give him a break," he said. "The man's left a clinic early and missed one of his classes. He'll probably show later."

"Well," she said, "I've got to tell Dr. Gregg."

Castel left as she tapped on the door to Gregg's office. Hank didn't want to become involved with Professor Costin's role in the Feldman case.

They picked up Professor Costin on the train to Brussels the next morning just before it crossed the Belgian border. Mattei had learned that the professor had telephoned Brussels twice before leaving the clinic on Saturday. Quick work by the local gendarmerie confirmed that someone from the clinic had called Avignon to purchase a one-way ticket to Brussels. A special police alert message from Marseille had been relayed to all border crossing points. The detectives who'd found Costin asleep in an empty compartment told Bastide he'd come along like a lamb. Now, after a quick flight from Lille, the professor looked more like a disheveled crane. Bastide hadn't had much sleep, but the excitement of the chase and the promise of results after so much frustration had kept both him and Mattei working efficiently and tirelessly all night.

Mattei was standing by the door speaking with one of the detectives from Lille who'd escorted Costin back to Marseille.

"Babar," Bastide called to him, "send Lenoir down for coffee and some *tartines.*" He turned to Costin. "You hungry?"

Costin shook his head. "Very well"—Bastide signaled to Mattei to shut the door—"let's get started."

Costin raised his long, thin hand. "May I say something?"

Bastide sat back in his chair and nodded. "Go ahead."

Costin spoke with his voice lowered, as if in a confessional. "I want you to know," he said rapidly, "that I had nothing to do with the Feldman girl's death. I left Aix because I could not become involved. I had trouble before . . . with a young girl."

Mattei and Bastide exchanged glances.

"It was in 1979 in Toul. I was fired for . . . ah, for taking liberties." Costin ran an unsteady right hand over his head as if he still had hair that needed smoothing.

"Don't misunderstand me," he explained, meeting Bastide's eyes for the first time since he'd entered his office. "I did nothing to the girl. She was willing. I mean . . . it was sex, not an attack of any kind. I don't believe in violence."

"But she was very young?" Bastide prompted.

"Yes," Costin replied, looking away again.

Lenoir pushed open the door, carrying a tray loaded with steaming espresso cups and a plate of buttered *tartines.* He put the tray on Mattei's desk and offered a *tartine* to Bastide. Bastide took one and bit into it, chewing slowly, watching Costin.

"Professor," he finally said, "we know all about your problem in Toul. We knew about it before you decided to leave Aix."

"But how?" Costin seemed confused.

Bastide rose and walked to Mattei's desk. He picked up a cup and sipped the strong coffee. "That, Professor, is not important," he said. "We don't give a damn what happened in Toul. We're interested in what happened in Aix. What happened to Mademoiselle Feldman? Is that why you decided to run after we had already warned you on the telephone that no one at Willington was to leave? That is what interests us at the moment."

Costin glanced at the tray. There was an extra cup.

"Here," Mattei said, handing it to him. "It's for you."

Costin managed to see the irony of the situation as he lifted the cup. In his revolutionary youth, he had often imagined being interrogated by the police for political reasons. It had never happened. He'd been hit with a club once during a Paris demonstration, but that had been an impersonal accident. Now he *was* being questioned by the police and, try as he could, he couldn't muster up the same strong sentiments or memorable words so many of his political heroes had managed while in police custody. He knew why. His was a sordid, common interrogation. It had nothing to do with politics. He smiled bitterly.

"You find something amusing in our questioning?" Bastide asked.

Costin shook his head. "No, I'm laughing at myself."

"I'm glad to see you have a sense of humor," Bastide told him, putting aside his coffee and preparing to light a cigar. "You're going to need it. You see, Professor, you're our number-one suspect."

"I left because I couldn't stand another scandal," Costin said. "It would mean the end of my career. I wouldn't be able to teach . . ." His voice trailed off.

"You're not making sense," Bastide told him. "You were running for Belgium. You knew everyone here would want to know why. You knew the Toul episode would eventually be known. What is this shit you're trying to sell us?"

"I was confused . . . afraid."

"It seems more likely you knew we'd come looking for you, once we found out about Toul, about your preference for the young ones. Then we'd find out about your weakness for Mademoiselle Feldman, your 'feelings' for her as a student; your gift of a poetry volume?" Bastide made an imperceptible sign of the head to Mattei, who stepped forward to replace him.

"When the Feldman girl refused you," Mattei said softly, "you were furious. Isn't that right?"

Costin's head jerked up, his mouth opened in astonishment. "You're mad! I didn't touch her," he shouted. "I won't be spoken to like this."

"Oh, yes you will," Mattei replied, still speaking calmly. "Please recall that you have not been invited to the hôtel de police for a simple questioning. You were just picked up trying to leave the country. A fugitive about to be charged with the murder of a mere child."

Costin turned toward Lenoir, seeking some sign of sympathy or support. The young detective lifted the tray. "Would you like a *tartine?*" he asked the professor, blank-faced. Bastide stifled a smile.

"Inspecteur Bastide," Costin said, his voice almost breaking, "I must have a lawyer and I would like to see Dr. Gregg. Also, my baggage . . . I want to shave."

"I'll do what I can," Bastide replied. "For the moment, I'd like you to go with Sous-Inspecteur Lenoir. He'll see to your immediate needs and ask you to fill out some forms."

Lenoir ushered Costin out of the office in silence. Bastide blew two perfect smoke rings toward the ceiling and sighed.

"Well," he asked Mattei, "what do you think?"

Mattei sat down heavily and pushed the tray aside. "I think he's our pigeon. Notice how he won't look you in the eye? The bastard!"

"I certainly hope he is," Bastide said, taking his jacket off the back of his chair. "I'd better go up and tell Aynard before he hears about it from Madame de Rozier. See that Costin does have access to a lawyer. God knows what the reaction will be from the Willington people. I only wish we had more on him."

"What more can Aynard ask?" Mattei replied.

Bastide stubbed out his cigar in a chipped glass ashtray. "Well,

Aynard may not be so happy. You see, he was hoping we'd put the collar on some poor outsider, preferably a North African worker. He is convinced that educators don't commit murders." Bastide paused at the door.

"Babar, I want you to take the professor over the hurdles again from the beginning. Start with his arrival in Aix, his work, his contacts, his love life and the details of his relationship with Mademoiselle Feldman. Put the heat on about where he was and what he was doing the night of her death. Shake him up a little."

"You can count on me, Roger. We'll be able to close this dossier in twenty-four hours."

Bastide frowned, straightening his tie. "Babar," he said, "I only hope you're right."

CHAPTER V

Bastide was lying on his back, arms behind his head, wide awake. The familiar noises of early morning rose from the Quai de Rive Neuve: delivery trucks passing on the wet pavement, cases of bottles being unloaded, the low roar of the first buses and the metallic rattle of shop fronts being raised. Janine was sleeping face down, only a stray wisp of dark hair showing above the *duvet*. They'd had a quiet, simple dinner in the apartment. Bastide had grilled a small pork roast and accompanied it with *lentilles au jus*. They'd rounded off their meal with a Camembert Janine had picked up at the market and a second bottle of Côte Rôtie.

Bastide turned toward Janine, smiling. Their lovemaking had been slow and satisfying. They'd both been asleep before midnight. He felt relaxed and ready for the office, Commissaire Aynard and the Feldman case. He turned back to contemplating the ceiling. The rain had increased. It was drumming on the roof tiles, pattering on the balcony. He was vaguely troubled by Professor Costin. The man was either very clever or very innocent. Bastide had been wrong before, but he usually could gauge a suspect's sincerity under questioning. Babar Mattei seemed to have no doubts of Costin's guilt, but Babar had a tendency to lose patience if a case became complicated or dragged on too long.

Janine murmured softly and turned toward him, her mouth slightly open. He hesitated for a moment, thinking of the warm pleasures of morning lovemaking, but he decided to let her sleep. He yawned and slid out of bed slowly, being careful not to disturb her. He showered and shaved, trimmed his thick black mustache and weighed himself. He'd put on a kilo. He promised himself he'd begin swimming at least twice a week at the Cercle Sportif. Aynard was a stickler for physical fitness among his detectives. He'd harassed Babar to the point where the chunky Corsican had actually stopped eating pasta. Bastide didn't want to let himself open to any criticism from Aynard. Particularly since the commissaire was right. You didn't survive on the street if you couldn't move fast.

He dressed quickly, pulling on the wrinkled tweed suit he'd worn the day before and knotting a blue tie Janine had given him on his last birthday. He went into the kitchen to put on his coffee and watched the Vieux Port from the window. The rain was slanting down into the calm gray water, kicking up a myriad of tiny splashes. The decks and cabins of the fishing boats and yachts moored along the quai shone from the dampness. Headlights from the morning traffic threw jagged, changing patterns of orange light over the soaked streets. Pedestrians were hurrying to work under tilted umbrellas.

He ate an orange, dropping the peelings into the sink, still staring at the Port. Mireille Peraud entered his mind without warning. Perhaps the thought of the Cercle Sportif had done it. He was vaguely troubled that Mireille's image often came to him after he'd made love to Janine. Now, in that state of mental suspension between waking and morning coffee, he relaxed and gave in to his fantasy. Bastide pictured her at the Cercle pool, bikini-clad and picking at a yogurt. Even against the morning's backdrop of gray rain, he could clearly see her flirtatious smile, the odalisque of her honey-brown body, the soft curve of her hip and the taut roundness of her breasts.

"*Assez, conard!*" he said to himself. "Enough." He poured out a small cup of thick black coffee, forcing Mireille from his mind. But even as he began to review the facts in the Feldman murder, he was aware that sooner or later he'd have to make a decision about her.

The rain was still pounding down when he clipped the holstered .38 to his belt and put on his trench coat and a corduroy cap. There was no use trying for a cab in such weather. He tiptoed back into the bedroom to telephone the hôtel de police for a duty car.

Madame de Rozier was lecturing Dr. Gregg and he didn't like it. He sat perched on the edge of a chair in front of her desk, feigning deep interest and understanding.

"As I told you before," she said sternly, "neither your program nor the university can allow such events to continue. When I heard that Professor Costin was in police custody I was thoroughly shocked."

Dr. Gregg nodded with understanding, but if Madame de Rozier had been able to read his mind she would have been more than shocked. He was imagining a riposte that was neither gentlemanly nor academic. "Kiss my ass, you old bitch!" That would have stopped her, he thought; probably drop her on the spot with a coronary.

"Of course, I immediately called Commissaire Aynard, an old friend, and asked for further information," she continued. "Information that you obviously don't have. It seems your so-called professor has a dark history of sexual offenses. Did you know that?"

Gregg cleared his throat. "No, madame," he said solemnly, "I did not."

She blew some air between her thin lips and shook her head.

"I don't know what your hiring criteria are, but they are obviously not adequate."

"I made inquiries through the university," Gregg said defensively. "His qualifications were in order. No one had anything negative to say about him."

She touched her puff of lifeless hair with quick little jabs, teasing it back into place. "The rector is most upset. So am I. You must realize, Dr. Gregg, that this scandal reflects on my office and on me personally."

"I know, and I assure you I am very sorry."

"That's all very well, but I do not see how the damage can be repaired. I do not believe you're a good administrator."

"Madame," Gregg replied, his voice rising in anger. "Please remember that I am not a young teaching assistant." He rose from the chair, struggling to control his temper. "I must return to my office."

She regarded him coldly, her black eyes mere slits in her heavily powdered face. "But, of course. I understand. I have nothing further to say. *Au revoir*, Dr. Gregg."

Now you've done it, he told himself as he left Madame de Rozier's office. She'd goaded him into losing his temper, and he knew she'd never forget it.

Dr. Gregg walked through the rainswept streets of Aix with his head down. He was in a black mood when he entered his office. Marcia Chappel was waiting for him. Her face was pale. Her breath smelled of cognac. "Thank God you're here," she said. "I tried to call you at Madame de Rozier's office."

"Well, what is it?" he snapped.

"It's Jean Bates."

"Oh, for God's sake, what's she done now?"

"She's missing."

He put his hands palms down on his desk and leaned forward, trying to compose himself. "That girl," he said slowly, "is a junkie; she sleeps around; she never goes to class; she flunks all her exams. She is permanently missing even when she's present. I should have sent her home long ago."

"No one's seen her for three days. She hasn't been back to her apartment. I . . . I have an awful feeling . . ."

"Calm down," he told her. "She's probably run off with someone."

"We'll have to notify her parents," Marcia Chappel said. "Maybe they can tell us something. Perhaps she decided to go home on her own."

"Not so fast." He took off his heavy spectacles and rubbed his eyes. "Let's give her another twenty-four hours. I've just had a clash with Madame de Rozier. It was unfortunate but inevitable . . . the old bitch!"

Marcia Chappel winced visibly at Gregg's language, but she felt sorry for him. She would have liked to put her arms around him, to offer some comfort, but she had more bad news.

"Four of our students are withdrawing," she said, unwilling to look him in the eye. "Their parents read about the Feldman murder. There was evidently an AP story out of Paris rehashing some of the recent French newspaper coverage."

Gregg dropped his thin frame into his desk chair and shook his head. "Marcia," he said quietly, using her first name for the first time, "I'm beginning to wonder if it's all worthwhile."

The next day was dry and surprisingly warm. The rain clouds had swept northeast toward the Alps, and a bright sun etched the hills of Provence with special clarity. The *autoroute* out of Marseille was packed with traffic as day-trippers and weekenders headed for the countryside to visit relatives, lunch at an auberge or pick mushrooms. The colors of Mont Sainte Victoire changed as the sun climbed higher into the blue sky.

A number of cars were already parked by the side of the winding road to Tholonet. Scouting parties of eager children were searching for picnic sites while their parents unloaded the folding chairs, food containers and wine bottles. Farther from the road, near the base of the mountain, a group of apprentice rock climbers were listening to their instructor explain the rudiments of handholds and wedges. They were members of a regional club, and their blue minibus had been driven as close to the mountain as possible. Two young male members had been assigned to carry the large, loaded ice chest. Puffing from the effort, they put the chest down and watched the first climbers edge hesitantly up the cliff face.

"Get it out of the sun," the tanned instructor called to them. "Find a cave."

They followed his orders, carrying it closer, peering at the jumble of fallen rocks and pine stumps at the base of the mountain.

"There," one of them said. "Over behind that brown boulder. It looks like an entrance."

They struggled on through the ash-like sand, dragging their heavy load till they reached the cave. The entrance was low. They had to kneel down to push the ice chest out of the sun. The sand was damp and soft.

"Here," one of them said, "I'll have to get inside to pull." He crawled forward on his hands and knees. The cold water falling from the cave's vault spattered his neck.

A strong odor stopped him cold. He almost choked as it filled his nostrils and assailed his throat. He blinked till his eyes became accustomed to the semidarkness. Then he saw it: a bare foot protruding from a mound of sand about fourteen inches from his face.

"*Bon Dieu!*" he gasped, his stomach turning over.

"What's going on?" his companion called from outside.

He backed out of the cave slowly, bile rising in his throat. He put his hand on his friend's shoulder, bracing himself, and spat onto the sand, trying to clear his mouth of an odor that had now become a taste.

"In there," he finally said, his hand shaking, "someone . . . is dead."

A rough half circle of uniformed policemen kept the curious at a distance. It was almost noon. Bastide crouched by the sand-caked corpse, holding a handkerchief over his nose and mouth. The girl had been strangled with her bra. Her swollen, disfigured throat bulged over the tightened straps. Her blond hair was alive with black ants. The attendant from the police morgue continued to brush delicately at the damp sand. As he cleared the face, Bastide cursed quietly. The individual puncture wounds were raised and raw, accentuated by the damp, clinging sand. They looked like the eruptions of some medieval plague. The brush moved from the forehead to the eye sockets. She'd been stabbed in each eye by the same thin weapon.

"Look at this," the attendant murmured. "The mouth . . . it's full of sand."

Bastide moved closer. At first he thought the sand had come from the hasty, unfinished burial. But now he could see he was wrong. The murderer had tamped the sand into the mouth till it was packed hard.

"*Le salaud!*" Bastide remarked, standing up and turning to Lenoir, who stood a short distance off, pale and uneasy.

"Lenoir," Bastide ordered, "stay with the corpse. You can ride to the morgue in their van. Dr. Colona will meet you there."

Lenoir nodded, still staring at the corpse, while the attendant continued his careful brushing. He had cleaned the flaccid breasts, uncovering new wounds as he moved slowly toward the hips.

"*Oh là là!*" the attendant remarked, turning toward Bastide. "Inspecteur, we've got a real crazy on our hands."

Just below the first wisps of pubic hair, the skin had been punctured by so many blows the flesh resembled chopped meat. Lenoir grimaced and turned away. Bastide felt a flash of sickness and revulsion. Dinh Le had said killing a young woman was like stamping on a flower. This was worse.

The attendant, the same man who'd assisted Bastide and Mattei on their last visit to the police morgue in Aix, finished his job. He stood up, putting the brush in the deep pocket of his gray gown and shaking sand from his hands.

"Let's go," he said to the policemen with the litter. "Let's get her on ice quickly."

"I'll come with you," Lenoir said.

"Good, always appreciate company." The attendant glanced down the hill toward the small group of onlookers that included family groups with their young children. Bastide followed his gaze.

"Send some uniforms down ahead of you," he told Lenoir, "and break that up." He watched the police lift their load. A lifeless arm slid off the litter and dragged in the sand as they started down the hill. Bastide took a few quick steps to catch up with them and lifted the arm, laying it back beside the body.

"Lenoir," he shouted, "tell Guignon I won't be eating with him today. I'll see him later." Bastide watched the forensic team slide into the entrance to the cave with their metal cases. He had planned to have lunch in Aix, but he knew he wouldn't be able to swallow a thing. He turned to survey the surrounding countryside, noting the nearby farms and summer homes. He'd have to check each one of them and interview their owners and inhabitants. He remembered Costin as he walked back toward the cave. He may have lost his job, he thought, but he is one very lucky professor.

The minstrel was sitting on a bench, his rucksack and guitar case beside him, watching a peacock strut back and forth in its enclosure. There were other birds on view, but he was fascinated by the play of color in the peacock's tail.

Now, as he raised the half-empty bottle of cognac to his lips, he had to concentrate to remember where he was. He knew it was a zoo, but he wasn't sure where it was or why he'd come there. The world around him was blurred on its edges. His blue eyes looked beyond the cages and foliage to the buildings and rooftops lining the nearby street.

It came to him slowly. He was in Marseille. Now he remembered. He'd been there for a few days. He'd left the cabin in Tholonet the day after Jean Bates had visited him. He'd stayed

with a friend on the rue d'Aix in the North African quarter and
he'd been continually high. He unbuttoned his stained field jacket
to take advantage of the winter sun. Now he was coming down out
of the clouds. His mind was working on the reason for leaving Aix.
Someone had told him that the best and cheapest hashish could be
found on the rue d'Aix. He smiled to himself. They were right.
But how did he come to the zoo? That puzzled him. Then the
mental fog dissipated. He'd been fired from his job. That was it!
He remembered the foreman telling him to get out of the icehouse;
the other workmen watching as he was pushed toward the exit. He
knew he'd laughed throughout. A clerk had handed him some
money and he'd stood outside still laughing as they'd slammed the
door. He'd gone back to his friend's room, picked up his guitar and
taken a bus. He hadn't known where it was going, but he'd seen
the zoo and decided to get off. He felt better now. He examined the
contents of his pockets slowly and methodically. He came up with
one bent joint of hash and two 50-franc notes.

"Shit!" he said aloud. He put the joint in a breast pocket of his
jacket and drank again from the bottle. The uncertain coughing
call of a lion reached him from another sector of the zoo, but he
ignored it. He was still making a special effort to think.

Marseille was no good for his kind of work. He remembered
trying his luck down at the Vieux Port, singing and playing near
the restaurants on the Quai du Port. The *Marseillais* were nig-
gardly. Only a few lonely coins in his guitar case after an hour of
effort. Then there'd been the kids. Skinny, rodent-faced gypsies
who'd sung along with him. He'd thought they were fun until
they'd ripped him off, running away with what little change he'd
made.

He ran his fingers through his long blond hair in a strangely
feminine gesture. His hair was snarled and sticky. He put his
hands palms down on his thighs. His fingernails were edged with
dirt. "Dirty boy," he murmured in German, "little pig." Another
drink and he decided to go back to Aix. At least he could keep
clean at the cabin and earn enough on the Cours Mirabeau to eat
regularly.

He pushed his thin frame upright on the bench. A negative
thought wrinkled his brow. He couldn't go back to the cabin. It

would not be a good thing to return to Tholonet. He waited while
the dulled, confused signals in his brain made their slow connection. It was the girl. The American. She'd taken the cabin from
him. He could never go there again. It was always an American
who caused trouble. It had begun with Sergeant Warren when he'd
been much younger. He'd become Otto Rupert Warren when his
mother had married the sergeant. He and his mother had been
close before the sergeant appeared. Then she'd only had time for
the stocky man in the tight uniform. She'd become his whore. The
minstrel's body seemed to tighten, and his dull eyes came alive as
he remembered listening to their rutting night after night. The
creak of the bed in the room next to his, the murmurs and cries of
his mother as the American drove into her again and again.

"My dearest mother," he murmured bitterly, recalling the day
she left Germany and left him. He took another long pull at the
bottle, held it up and shook the few inches of cognac left.

He would have to watch his money now to save enough for the
bus to Aix. He would put the cabin out of his mind. If he couldn't
go back to Tholonet, he'd find a room in Aix. The American girl
had been very clever. She'd called him the minstrel. He'd liked
that. But it was all a sham. He'd seen through her as he'd seen
through the other one. The one who'd smiled at him each time
she'd passed him on the Cours. The one with the long legs and the
dark hair he'd surprised in the shower. He'd punished them both,
and the stupid Sergeant Warren and his slut of a mother could do
nothing about it.

Detective Jean Lenoir often wondered what made him stay in
the police. His contemporaries had good jobs in banks and travel
agencies or worked as salesmen. Most of them were married and
settled down with families. His life was quite different. The fact
that he hadn't been promoted in so long had dampened his enthusiasm. His morale was waning steadily each day like a slow leak. If it
hadn't been for Mattei's encouragement, he would have submitted
his resignation months ago.

As he jumped down from the concrete loading platform of the
Glacière de Midi, the thought of laying his walking papers on the
desk of a surprised Commissaire Aynard was especially appealing.

He'd spent the day visiting icehouses and freezer establishments in and around Marseille. He still wasn't finished, but he was already bored. He stood by the small police sedan and curled the tips of his drooping mustache, looking off toward the industrial port. A gray freighter flying a Dutch flag was moving along the Digue du Large, gliding effortlessly toward the open sea under a cluster of noisy gulls. He pictured himself standing on the bridge as a ship's officer bound for far lands and exotic ports. The ship disappeared behind a loading dock, and he slid behind the wheel of the police car.

He had another call to make just outside the dock area. It was a small icehouse specializing in the packing and shipment of shellfish. He was sure he'd caught a cold. He could feel a tingling in his sinuses. What other detective in Marseille had spent the last twenty-four hours walking in and out of icehouses? None. He knew that. He drove down along a chain-link fence and turned out onto the two-lane road to Carry le Rouet. There was very little traffic. Most normal people were still enjoying their long lunches. He'd munched a sandwich of *saucisson sec* in a bar on the Boulevard de Dunkerque. The draft beer he'd ordered had tasted like soap suds, and the beetle-browed *patron* had made him feel like an interloper . . . as if he'd recognized him as a *flic* and wanted to make sure he didn't return.

He speeded up, anxious to finish his day and return to the office. The sun was fading, and some ominous black clouds were drifting in from the Mediterranean. He almost missed the turnoff to the ice plant, but he braked quickly and spun the wheel, screeching into a rutted road leading to a low cinder-block building. A yellow sign with black letters hung over the entrance to the office. He checked his notes. J. Magabian was the proprietor. It matched the sign. He parked, slammed the door and climbed the three wooden stairs to the office door.

Monsieur Magabian was drinking tea from a glass. His desk was a litter of correspondence and order forms dominated by family photos in plastic frames. Lenoir introduced himself, showed his credentials and accepted an offer to sit down. Magabian was huge. His dark hair stood up like a wire brush, his stomach overflowed his belt.

"There is a problem?" Magabian said, his brown spaniel eyes humble and concerned.

"No, I don't think so," Lenoir told him reassuringly. "I . . ." he searched into his jacket and gingerly produced the long ice pick that had already put a hole in his wallet pocket.

"Do you use these here?" he asked.

Magabian nodded. "Yes, we do, to break up the slabs for feeding into the crushing machine. But not for long. I've ordered a mechanical system from Italy. Electricity does all the work."

"How many people do you employ?"

"At the moment we have ten. Excuse me, Monsieur . . . ?"

"Lenoir."

"Yes, Monsieur Lenoir. Why are you asking me all this? Perhaps if you tell me what you are looking for?"

"We believe this type of pick was used as a murder weapon."

"How bizarre! But surely, you must have more information? Anyone can procure a long pick, bought or stolen. I would say your search could go on forever."

Lenoir agreed. "It is difficult, but we've got to keep trying."

Magabian murmured in sympathy. "Surely, I will help you if I can. Do you want to speak to my employees? Let me tell you, I can vouch for them. Most of them are family members."

Forty-five minutes later, Lenoir closed his notebook, thanked the last worker he'd interviewed and walked through the frosty interior of the noisy plant. He knew his notes were useless. He was sure of one thing. He'd think twice before eating a mussel or clam iced under Magabian's auspices. The day's work had been a waste of time. Each icehouse had produced a staff of obvious innocents: hardworking family men and women with simple tastes and needs totally unconnected with the dead students in Aix. He paused for a minute before leaving the plant floor and checked his notes. Could he have missed something? His nose was beginning to run from the cold. Frustrated, he entered the warmth of Magabian's office.

During Lenoir's absence, Magabian had been struggling with his conscience. If he told the detective about the German boy he'd fired, he could be in trouble for hiring someone without a work permit. If he didn't mention it, the police might come back and he would be under suspicion for harboring a criminal. Detective Lenoir seemed a sympathetic person, he reasoned, not like a *real* policeman. Magabian made his decision. As Lenoir entered, he insisted the detective sit down again.

"There is one point I had forgotten," Magabian told him. "We had a German boy working here for a few weeks. I fired him two days ago. He was on drugs. A danger to all around him. I can't have that here."

Lenoir forgot his runny nose. "Do you have his name and address?"

"He must have filled out a form for the payroll. Wait one minute and I'll look." Magabian got up and opened a drawer in a dented file cabinet. He licked his stubby fingers and began probing through a sheaf of papers. "We paid him off that morning," he said over his shoulder. "The fool just laughed when we put him out the door. Laughed and laughed. Ah, here it is." He lumbered back to his desk and put on his bifocals, holding the sheet of paper at a distance.

"Otto Rupert," Magabian read, "domiciled in Aix. No further address and no telephone. He was a skinny blond fellow with long hair."

Lenoir rose and took the paper out of Magabian's hand, his eyes drawn to the small, tight signature at the bottom of the form. "Monsieur Magabian," he said, "this changes everything. I'm afraid I'll have to talk to your workers again."

Magabian gestured to the door leading to his plant. "If it will help . . ."

As Lenoir braved the cold again, he remembered that both Bastide and Mattei had referred to the first solid lead in a case as a "whiff of shit." For the first time in his career, Lenoir knew what they meant.

Bastide waited impatiently under the high domed ceiling of the Gare Saint Charles. The train for Valence, Lyon and Paris was about to pull out, and late travelers were running along the concrete quai, dragging their baggage, frantically seeking their assigned cars. The wind whistled through the cavernous entrance to the station, blowing candy and sandwich wrappers onto the tracks. The concourse was a crowded bedlam of unintelligible loudspeaker announcements, honking baggage vans and the rumble of idling diesel locomotives. A high-speed train had just pulled in and its passengers were pouring toward the exits and taxi ramps.

Bastide buttoned the collar of his trench coat and glanced at his watch. The train from Arles was four minutes late. His mother was paying one of her rare visits to Marseille, and he'd insisted on taking her to lunch after her arrival. She very rarely left the small *mas* near Arles, but there was a legal question involved in some old family property at Le Vallon des Auffes and she had come in to see Maître Jeannot, her solicitor.

He walked farther out along the quai designated for the Arles arrival. Far off in the gray drizzle, he could see an approaching yellow light. Then the slow-moving engine came in sight, followed by the caterpillar of passenger cars. The throbbing engine finally slid by him and came to a halt. He positioned himself for a clear view of the debarking passengers, eager for his first sight of her in two months. At her time of life, each separation seemed to accelerate the aging process. He knew it was inevitable, but it always made him feel a certain guilt.

She was one of the first out of the train, taking her time, oblivious to the impatience of the passengers crowding the car's exit behind her. Bastide hurried toward her. She was wearing an old astrakhan coat and carrying a black umbrella. A young man handed down her one piece of baggage. She had begun to rearrange her bun of gray hair when Bastide tapped her lightly on the shoulder and took her in his arms.

"Madame Bastide," he greeted her, "welcome to Marseille!" They kissed each other on both cheeks.

"*Pardi,*" he told her, "you do look chic. I'm surprised Monsieur Fontet allowed you to leave."

"*Eh, mon petit,*" she laughed, "Fontet is becoming senile. But I didn't come here to talk about him. Tell me about you."

He picked up her bag and began the same banal recital that marked each of their meetings. As they walked to the exits, he told her about his dinner for the Matteis, his most recent visit to the Cercle Sportif, a humorous aspect of a noncase involving a kitchen stained with beef blood belonging to an illegal butcher. He examined her as he talked. She'd retained her countrywoman's tan.

Her eyes were lively, taking in all around her. She moved a bit slowly, but her grip on his arm was strong. He glanced at her legs. They were encased in dark, utilitarian stockings. He noticed that one ankle seemed slightly swollen.

"Tell me," he asked solicitously, "do you have trouble walking?"

"It's nothing. The doctor scolded me for climbing the oak hill. A slight sprain, but that's all over."

"Until you do it again!" Bastide admonished her. "Really, Mother, you're sometimes very difficult."

"The best mushrooms are there. You know that."

"And you're not wearing a hat."

"*Tant pis.*" She shrugged. "I've got my umbrella. That's enough, Roger! I didn't come here to be lectured. Where are we going for lunch?"

"We have a table at the Calypso. I thought you'd enjoy that. It's right on the sea."

"Is it expensive?"

"Of course not," he lied. "But they have some of the best fish in Marseille."

She shrugged, unimpressed. "We could have had something to eat at your apartment. That would have been fine with me."

"Well, we're eating at the Calypso, so relax and enjoy it."

She didn't relax. She never did in a restaurant. A master of Provençal cuisine herself, she was both curious and critical when it came to eating out. She eyed the smiling maître d'hôtel with suspicion as he seated them by a seaside window, and openly scrutinized the neighboring tables to see what was being served. Years ago, her attitude might have embarrassed Bastide. Now it only amused him.

"I'll just have some *soupe de poisson*," she announced, watching a stout businessman across from them crack a lobster claw.

"One moment," Bastide said, holding up his hand, "you can have your fish soup, but you will also share the fresh *loup de mer* I've already ordered. We'll have it grilled with fennel, the way you like it." He made a quick sign to one of the white-jacketed waiters. Within seconds, he'd brought the entire fish on a tray for their inspection. Its eyes were clear and its skin glistened with freshness. When the *loup* was whisked away to the grill, Bastide ordered a glass of port and a pastis. He also asked that a bottle of **Blanc de Blancs** be brought to the table in an ice bucket.

"So," he asked, gesturing toward the window, "do you like the view?"

She squinted, surveying the white-capped sea, the plunging gulls and the bulky towers of the Château d'If. "It's beautiful," she admitted. "That was your father's kingdom."

Bastide agreed, remembering the busy mornings he'd spent helping his father in the bobbing double-ended fishing boat.

"He loved it out there," she told Bastide. "He always came back in a good mood. Remember how he'd save the best *rouget* for us? How we'd grill them outside on the terrace?"

He did remember. It hurt him to think how lives change with time. It had been another world and he'd been another person. He watched an incoming trawler sink its bow into the spray. At least, he told himself, it had been a happy time. Their drinks came and they toasted each other. He took her tanned, heavy-veined hand and squeezed it.

"How is your lady friend?" she murmured, sipping her port.

"Fine," he replied, always unprepared to cope with her query, never knowing when it would come.

He hadn't intended to mention Janine to his mother when they first met, but shortly after they'd begun their liaison, his mother had picked up the news on her own. It wasn't far from Marseille to Arles. Her old friends at Le Vallon des Auffes saw to it that she was informed. He'd never mentioned the circumstances of his first meeting with Janine or the fact that she'd been in a less than honorable occupation. He preferred to cloak their relationship in a haze of uncertainty.

"I'd like to meet her sometime. Bring her to the *mas*."

"One of these days," he promised without enthusiasm, noting the I'll-believe-that-when-I-see-it nod from his mother.

The waiter put a bowl of *rouille*, a silver-topped container of grated cheese and a plate of toasted croutons on their table for the *soupe de poisson*. His mother dipped a crouton into the *rouille* sauce, tasting it.

"Not enough garlic," she commented.

"They have a lot of foreign customers," he chided her. "We all know you're the best cook in the Midi. Give the other professionals a chance."

"Well," she said, draining her glass of port, "these young chefs have a lot to learn."

When the steaming, fragrant *soupe de poisson* was served, she nodded her approval before tasting it.

"I can tell it's good," she said. "Not a gruel of bones, not too much saffron."

They dotted their soup with croutons, spotted them with generous helpings of *rouille* and mounded them with a snowfall of cheese. They ate in silence, enjoying their meal. Bastide filled their glasses with Blanc de Blancs.

"You know, *Maman,*" he finally said, wiping his mouth, "I worry about you up there at the *mas.* Aren't you lonely?"

"Not at all," she replied. "I have Prosper and my neighbors."

"Prosper is the oldest Labrador in France, and your neighbors would sleep through the second coming of Christ."

She put down her spoon, her dark eyes flashing. "Well, what would you suggest? That I move in with you in your tiny apartment?"

"We've been through this before," he said gently.

"Oh, have we? If you mean that charming little walled estate in Saint Rémy where they lock up all the old people, the answer is no."

"But it's not that at all. It's open, airy and full of interesting boarders. One of Babar's uncles was there. He was very happy until . . ."

"Until he croaked? That's it, isn't it? *Non, merci,* I'll stay at home in my own house, with my dog and my neighbors."

"*Ça va,*" he sighed. "Let's not argue about it."

"In addition," she continued, "can you imagine me without my garden? The blossoms in the spring, the birds and the hum of the cicadas? Then the figs and cherries, plums and peaches. *Non, chéri,* that's my life."

He nodded, smiling. "I know it is. I just worry about you."

"Don't," she said, drawing herself erect and brushing her bodice, glancing toward the serving area. "Very few cooks can ruin a *loup,* but too much grilling can dry it out."

"Don't worry," he told her, "the chef is a true professional."

The *loup* was perfect, firm and juicy, its skin barely marked by the grill. He was reassured to see his mother eat heartily, foraging the last bits of tender flesh from the bones. The wine had loosened her tongue, and she treated him to a full panoply of the latest gossip from Arles: the doings of the local officials, a scandal in the gendarmerie and her favorite myth, renewed annually, about Gypsies stealing her chickens. They had just begun their salad and Tomme cheese when the maître d'hôtel approached the table.

"Excuse me, Monsieur l'Inspecteur," he said quietly, "a telephone call."

It was Mattei. Bastide sensed the excitement in his voice.

"Lenoir may have found something in one of the *glacières*. I thought you'd want to know."

Bastide's first impulse was to rush back to his office. He glanced toward his mother, sitting by the window, gazing out to the sea. She seemed suddenly small and terribly alone. *"Eh bien,"* Bastide replied firmly, "you handle it for the moment. Have all the details ready for me. Don't let Lenoir out of your sight. I don't want Aynard buttonholing him in the corridor."

"I can give you the gist of his report—"

"No," Bastide said, "I'm in the middle of an important lunch."

"As you wish," Mattei responded. He heard the click of the receiver. "What the hell is he up to?" Mattei pondered, putting the telephone down.

The minstrel had had a lot of time to think. When the bus turned into the terminal, he had worked out a plan that would make it perfectly safe to stay in Aix. He found a cheap room in a hotel on the narrow rue de la Fonderie with a bath on the same floor. He reassured the elderly room clerk of his solvency by handing over one of the 50-franc notes. He bathed first and let his dirty clothes soak in the soapy, tepid water while he shaved. He eyed his shoulder-length blond hair critically in the cracked mirror. Then he pulled on a patched pair of gray slacks and a spotted white wool sweater. It took him half an hour to finish washing his dirty clothes, wring them out and clean the bathtub as instructed by the hand-lettered sign over the taps. He returned to his room, draped his damp clothes over the small, wheezing steam ventilator and sat down on the bed, rummaging through his rucksack.

He found the two passports. The German passport had been renewed not too long before. He flicked through it, pausing at the page bearing his photo. It presented Otto Rupert Warren as he now looked. He was wearing a headband, and his hair was long and unkempt. He smoothed the page and laid the German passport on the bed. The blue American passport was not as new. Sergeant Warren had insisted he apply for it before leaving him in Germany. At that time, he'd had close-cropped hair and he'd been a bit heavier. He was frowning in the photo. He remembered how the sergeant had stood behind the photographer, telling him to smile. He picked up the German passport, ripped out the photo of himself and tore the passport in half, stuffing the halves into his pocket. He put the American passport back into his rucksack and began to rip the German passport apart, page by page.

Walking to the barbershop near the Place du Marche, he dropped the remnants of his German passport into two separate refuse cans. He closed his eyes as the buzzing electric clipper rolled over his skull and his blond hair fell on the linoleum-covered floor. It was like a rebirth. A new life. Otto Rupert Warren, the street singer with an American father, now a citizen of the United States. At least the sergeant was useful for something. The gentle fingers of the barber brushed some hair from his forehead. The minstrel felt like dozing off, but he knew he'd have to get to work. When he'd paid for the haircut, he wouldn't have many francs left.

He suddenly remembered the ice pick. It was still in his guitar case back at the hotel. His eyes opened. He had been very careless. It should have been well hidden before he left the room. He would have to be more careful. He closed his eyes again as the barber put aside the clippers and began to massage his scalp. He was finding it easier to remember now. He saw Tholonet and the massive heights of Sainte Victoire. He recalled Jean Bates and their walk over the uneven ground. He was watching her as she leered at him, taking off her blouse, proudly exhibiting her heavy breasts. She'd had an unattractive roll of fat at her waist. She'd pulled him down beside her while she slipped out of her clothes, exposing her pink flesh, the dark nipples of her breasts and her wide thighs. She'd been insistent as her excitement increased.

He'd moved swiftly, talking all the time. "You're a bad girl," he'd said, watching her eyes widen in surprise.

"Hey!" she'd managed to say, "cut it out. That hurts."

"Bad girl! You have a foul mouth. You should eat sand."

"Stop!" she'd shouted, pushing back, trying to free herself. "You're crazy. Let me up!"

He'd pushed a handful of powdery sand into her open mouth. She'd choked, spitting and gagging. "American whore," he'd hissed, squeezing her nose till she opened her mouth again. "Filthy bitch. Eat the pure sand!"

One of her hands grabbed his throat. She'd fought with all her strength, her eyes reflecting pure terror. He'd reached behind him freeing the pick from under his sweater. The thin, round blade arced through the air.

"Shut your eyes!" he'd ordered striking at her. "Shut them, shut them, shut them!"

The life had gone out of her slowly as he'd stabbed her again and again. Finally, she'd made an acquiescent sound, like air being let out of a tire. Her bloodied body had jerked twice and lain still. When he'd finished, he'd cleaned the blade on some dried leaves. There had been a warm dampness at his crotch and spittle on his chin.

A shudder ran through him.

"You all right?" the barber asked, close to his ear.

"Yes," he replied, pushing himself straight in the chair. "Just a chill."

"Anything else? Some hair oil or tonic?"

"No," he replied, surveying his new self in the mirror. "That's just fine."

Hank Castel paced up and down outside the line of telephone booths in the main post office. He'd placed his call to New York twenty minutes earlier, but the grim woman behind the counter hadn't yet given him the nod. He had studying to do, and he wished he'd never agreed to call Ginnie's father. A tall Senegalese with blue-black skin was shouting in one of the booths. He was holding the phone away from his ear with long, thin fingers. Even with the booth's door closed, his voice boomed out, dominating the normal murmur and shuffle of the post office.

"But the check has not arrived!" the Senegalese yelled in measured French. "I don't think you've sent it. Oh no, my brother . . . I do *not* believe you."

Castel watched a gray-haired, elegant woman in a well-tailored gray suit carrying a small package to the counter. He caught the subtle fragrance of her perfume and found himself examining her figure with interest. It never failed to amaze him how middle-aged French women were able to remain so seductive.

"Monsieur Castel," the dour clerk called, "booth number 4."

He entered the booth, slid the door shut and lifted the receiver. He could hear the far-off buzzing. "We're trying your call to New York," an anonymous voice told him. A woman finally responded. "Go ahead," the operator said.

"Hello, Feldman & McMann."

"Is Mr. Feldman in? This is Hank Castel calling from France."

"One moment, please."

More buzzing and clicking. Then Feldman came on the line. "Hank? How are you? I've told my secretary to interrupt me no matter what when your calls come through. What's new?"

"I'm calling early this week. There's been a . . . new development."

"Go on," Feldman said eagerly.

"Another murder."

"Son of a bitch!" Feldman cursed. "Who was it?"

"Another student, Jean Bates. She used to room with your daughter."

There was a few seconds of silence. Castel could hear Feldman take a deep breath. "What the hell is going on over there?" he finally said. "Can't they protect those kids? It's a goddamn disgrace!"

"Everybody's uptight," Castel told him. "A lot of students are pulling out."

"I don't blame them," Feldman said. "What about the cops? What the hell are they doing? Must have their fingers up their asses."

"They're working on it," Castel said without much conviction. "Well, I did think you'd want to know."

"You're damn right. Listen, Hank, I think I better come over."

"Why?"

"Because I've got a big stake in what goes on, remember. I want to make sure they find Ginnie's murderer. It means a lot to me. You should understand that."

"I do, Mr. Feldman," Castel replied, wishing he could come up with an instant argument to convince Feldman to stay in New York. Nothing but trouble, he thought to himself, nothing but trouble.

"You get me a room . . . at that same hotel. Mrs. Feldman won't be with me, so make it a single, with bath."

"For how long?"

"How the hell do I know? Tell 'em a week, maybe two. We'll see how things go. And Hank, don't tell Dr. Gregg I'm coming over. I'd like to catch that inefficient bastard with his guard down. I may stop in Paris for a day. I've got a friend in the embassy. A little heat on those Keystone kops down there wouldn't hurt at this point."

"It'll be awkward for me," Castel said, "not telling Dr. Gregg."

"Not to worry. Just keep your mouth shut. Who knows we even talked? I read about it in the paper, right?"

"Well . . ."

"Relax, kid, I'll see that you're taken care of. Well, I've got to get organized. I'll call you from Paris."

"I don't have a telephone."

"Okay, keep checking with the hotel. I'll see you when I get there. What was the poor girl's name?"

"Bates, Jean Bates."

"Where was she from?"

Castel paused. "I think her parents live in Minneapolis."

"I'll try to contact them. I know how they must feel. Thanks for calling, Hank."

"But—" The phone went dead. As Castel hung up and walked to the counter to pay for the call, he understood why Feldman was so successful. Hank Castel hadn't signed any contract, but he already felt like he was working for him.

CHAPTER VI

Commissaire Aynard's ulcers were bothering him. He'd already taken two tablets, but they hadn't helped. He'd been on the phone to Paris about a troubling embezzlement case with repercussions in Marseille. A pillar of the local community and government supporter might be involved. The Ministry wanted Aynard to handle the investigation with delicacy. It was a problem he'd not had when he'd awakened that morning. But it wasn't the embezzlement that had prompted the first pains below his sternum. Just before ringing off, his superior in Paris had asked about the Feldman case, referring to it as the "Feldman-Bates murders." Aynard had explained Lenoir's find at the Magabian establishment, inferring the investigation was making considerable progress. The unimpressed silence on the other end of the line had not been encouraging.

"I'd suggest you move quickly," he'd been told. "The Minister referred to your situation at the staff meeting this morning. He said we'll have to consider a special student cemetery for the university if things continue as they are."

Aynard shot his cuffs, readjusted his spectacles and sighed. He was not happy with Bastide . . . not happy at all. He moved too slowly. When he did move, he was often indiscreet and heavy-handed. Aynard's wife had said it was a disgrace having an inspector on his staff who was carrying on an affair with the mistress of a prominent and respected businessman. Aynard could only agree, but she didn't realize how many influential friends Janine Bourdet had. The special citation Bastide had received for the McCallister case hadn't made things any easier. Aynard was about to call Bastide's office for the second time when Bastide tapped on the frosted glass of his door and walked into his office.

"Sorry to have taken so long," Bastide said. "I'm getting ready to check the farms and villas near the murder scene at Le Tholonet." Aynard gestured toward the chair in front of his desk. He brought his thin hands together under his chin, staring at Bastide. A twinge of pain jerked a corner of his mouth into what appeared to be a smile. Bastide watched him, slightly puzzled.

"*Mon cher* Bastide," Aynard began, "we are faced with a very serious situation. The McCallister case was different. Important, of course, but different. There we were dealing with the past, the war, old memories. Here, with these student murders, we are dealing with the future, the future and reputation of a great university. I've mentioned this before, but I'm not sure you fully understand. I *know* Mattei doesn't . . . but that's not important. I must be sure you, as the inspector responsible for the investigation, can see how essential it is for us to close the case successfully and soon." Aynard finished, nodded his head slightly, as if agreeing with his own words, and waited for a response.

Bastide would have preferred to tell Aynard that the case would be closed much sooner if he were not obliged to waste time listening to stupid lectures. Instead, he cleared his throat and told Aynard he was perfectly aware of the case's importance.

"As I said yesterday," Bastide continued, "Lenoir was able to pick up a good lead in Marseille, the best we've had so far. I'm sure we'll be able to do something with it."

"I hope you're correct," Aynard sighed. "I'm not that optimistic. You thought Professor Costin was your man. We all know how it turned out. Thank God, I wasn't tempted to inform Paris prematurely of that success! I've told you before, Inspecteur, I am ready to provide extra help if you need it. I know you're shorthanded. I could let you have someone from theft. Things are comparatively slow with them at the moment."

He's playing the same record, Bastide told himself. He'd like nothing better than to break up my team by infiltrating my section with one of those academic wonders full of psychological theories of how environment produces a criminal.

"No, thank you," Bastide replied. "My people can handle it."

"Somehow I knew you'd say that," Aynard said with a certain

amount of sarcasm. "All I can tell you is they better make a special effort."

"We are," Bastide told him, glaring across the desk.

Aynard returned his glare for a few seconds before picking up the notes from his telephone call. "Another subject," Aynard said. "You know Monsieur Jacques Rémy, don't you?"

Bastide smoothed his mustache before replying, trying to fathom the shallows of Aynard's purpose.

"Yes, I know of him. He's always mentioned in the press. He's also a crook."

A sudden pain caused Aynard to shift in his chair. He pictured his martyred stomach grinding and twisting into unnatural shapes under the assault of newly released acids.

"Why do you say that?" he asked through clenched teeth.

"Everyone in Marseille knows it. If it wasn't for the favors he's done a number of government officials, he'd be watching the sun set on the hills near Les Baumettes from a well-locked cell."

"That's all, Inspecteur," Aynard snapped.

Bastide stood up and walked toward the door, waiting for Aynard's traditional parting shot. It wasn't long in coming.

"Oh, Bastide," the Commissaire said, "you seem to have put on some weight. It may look good on a four-star chef; it doesn't on an inspecteur of Homicide. Perhaps you and your rotund friend Mattei could exercise together."

Bastide looked out over the valley from the terrace of a luxurious villa. The swimming pool was covered for the winter with a sheet of blue plastic. Mont Sainte Victoire was behind him. The woods to his front were sparse, dotted with stone-crowned hillocks and olive trees with gnarled, twisted trunks. The caretaker jabbed his garden shears at a distant tiled roof.

"That's the Junot house. He's in the Middle East working on some Arab project. He was here in September. His wife came down from Paris to spend some time with him. Childless couple. He must be making a fortune out there. No one's been in the house since then."

The caretaker paused to blow his nose in a stained handkerchief. He was a husky, silver-haired man dressed in old-fashioned blue work clothes. He'd come up from the far field when Bastide had driven onto the property. He appeared to be a good source of information.

"Over there—you can hardly see it—is the Tobler estate. He's a Swiss . . . or claims to be. I think he's Alsatian, but it's none of my business. Live and let live, I say. It's empty too. They show up in June and stay till August. He drinks, she sunbathes topless and the kids raise hell in Aix."

Bastide turned toward the turreted, stucco-covered towers of the villa. "And your employers . . . have they been here recently?"

"No, but they may decide to come down for Christmas. Monsieur is an art dealer and—"

"But no one has used the house recently?"

"No one."

"You've heard about the murder?"

"*Bien sur!* Everyone in Tholonet is talking about it. The work of a fiend. I hear he cut the girl into pieces and—"

"No," Bastide said emphatically, "that is not true." He turned back toward the panorama. He saw what looked like the corner of a roof hidden among some far-off pines.

"What's that?" he asked.

"Where?"

"Over there, closer to the mountain."

The caretaker squinted into the distance. "That's Antoine Grimaud's old *cabanon*. It's usually empty."

"Usually?"

"Antoine lives in Nice now, but his son Édouard uses it occasionally. I seldom get over in that direction."

"This Édouard, what does he do?"

"Nothing much. Spends the old man's money. Sometimes he lets his friends borrow the *cabanon*."

"Anyone lately?"

"Come to think of it, I did see some smoke over there the other day. Didn't give it much thought, though."

"Where can I find Édouard Grimaud?"

"He's off somewhere in the Far East or India with one of those gurus or whatever you call them."

It took Bastide ten minutes to pilot his police sedan through the pines and *garrigue* surrounding the isolated *cabanon*. He walked to the door, blowing on his hands to warm them.

"Anyone home?" he shouted. He pounded the door before he noticed it was secured from the outside with a small padlock. He shouted once more and glanced over his shoulder at the empty road before unleashing a kick that sent both the padlock and the hinge flying.

The *cabanon* was damp and redolent of mold. Bastide walked to the small stone sink to examine two upended wine glasses left to dry in its basin. He shook out his handkerchief and picked a glass up by the stem, sniffing. It had been washed. There was no clue to what it had held. He moved slowly through the room, running his hands over the rough blanket on the couch, looking under the cushions, poking in the fireplace and opening the cupboards. The hearth held old ashes and the fragments of some scorched logs. A busy spider had woven a web around the dried flowers on the windowsill, pulling them together in a desiccated peak of dull color. There were some newspapers in a wicker basket, copies of the Aix edition of *Le Méridional*. He checked the dates. They were more than six days old. He was about to throw them back when he noticed bits of paper at the bottom of the basket. He knelt down and grubbed through the crumpled scraps. A used bus ticket, a supermarket tally, an empty packet of Bastos cigarettes and a thin sheet of paper with figures on it, obviously a paycheck stub. He had trouble making out the company name stamped on the sheet. He held it up to the dim light from the dirty window. It was faint but legible. "J. Magabian," he read. A slow smile spread over his face as he stood up.

Commissaire Aynard was being unusually polite to Jean Lenoir. Aynard had waited for Bastide to leave his office the next day before ordering Lenoir up to the third floor.

"So," Aynard said, smiling, "all you really have to go on are the suppositions that this suspect is a young German, he has long blond hair, he's a junkie, he worked in a *glacière*, where he lost his job, and he resides in Aix."

"I think they're more than suppositions, sir," Lenoir replied, still pleased at having been invited to make a personal report to the Commissaire.

"Oh, you do?" Aynard's smile had a slight edge to it. "Inspecteur Bastide informs me you did a good job pinpointing this suspect."

"He did?" Lenoir beamed. "It was not too difficult."

"Yes," Aynard said, "I tend to agree with you. *Mon cher* Lenoir, do you realize how many blond, long-haired, dope-taking Germans are currently in France?"

"No sir."

"There are thousands of them."

"I see."

"Do you? That's very good."

Lenoir sensed that things were not going too well. His mind raced, trying to come up with some pertinent comment that would deflect Aynard from what now appeared to be another manifestation of his displeasure with the Homicide section.

"The two important links," Lenoir ventured, "are the ice pick and the German's residence in Aix."

"The ice pick? What ice pick?"

Lenoir looked surprised at the question. "The murder weapon," he said.

"Does the German have an ice pick? If he does, is it the murder weapon?"

"Well, he worked at a *glacière* . . ."

"Yes, Lenoir, I know. But butchers work with knives, pharmacists handle poison and hunters own shotguns. It doesn't make them suspects. As to Aix . . . every young vagabond in Europe squats there at some time in their travels. My point is that you only have a tenuous lead at best and I think Bastide is exaggerating its importance. Up to a point, as chief of Homicide, that's his business. But I do not want you to be misled by the unscientific methods sometimes used by Bastide and Mattei. In any case, I've enjoyed our little chat. I like to keep contact with our young detectives. It gives me a fresh viewpoint. I may call on you from time to time to tell me of your work in this case. Good day, Lenoir."

"Monsieur le Commissaire," Lenoir replied. Once outside, he

frowned. "The old bastard," he said to himself, surprised by his own lucidity. "He wants me to be his spy."

Dr. Gregg put the telephone down slowly. It was the fourth call he'd had since eleven o'clock in the morning. A correspondent from Agence France Presse had been first, posing painstaking questions about what he insisted on calling "the Willington murders." Gregg had tried to convince him that another journalistic label would be more appropriate. The other three calls had come from frantic parents in the United States. One hysterical mother had threatened to sue Willington University if her daughter wasn't put on the telephone immediately. Ten minutes of calming conversation had managed to appease her, but Gregg had promised that the girl would call home by nightfall. The other three calls were less emotional but just as catastrophic. Each one confirmed the withdrawal of another student. Each caller had demanded a refund. The fifth call caught Gregg as he slumped in his seat, massaging his tired eyes.

"Hello, Ron?" a hearty voice bellowed over mile after mile of transatlantic cable.

Gregg recognized President Carlton Bass's voice immediately. "Hello, Carlton," he replied, trying to sound friendly.

"Ron, I want you to know how much I sympathize with you. One hell of a situation! I've just come from a faculty meeting and everyone wants you to know how sorry they are. We're all behind you one hundred percent."

"Thanks, Carlton. That's very kind."

"Now, Ron . . ."

"Yes?"

"We think it would be wise to send a lawyer over there. Someone to advise you. Harley Cannon knows a fellow in Boston who's had experience in France and knows the language. He could be a big help to you. What do you say?"

Harley Cannon was the dean of law at Willington University. As far as Gregg was concerned, he was also a middle-aged nincompoop. Anyone he recommended was sure to be a disaster. Gregg had little choice.

"That sounds fine, Carlton," he replied. "Has this lawyer had experience in criminal cases?"

There was a pause as the president conferred with someone. Obviously Cannon was standing beside him. "It's not really important, Ron," Bass finally replied. "The main thing is to have solid legal advice."

"Yes, I understand. We haven't had any real problems yet. Perhaps we should wait a few days . . ."

Gregg could hear someone speaking in the background and Bass replying. "You can't trust the French in legal matters," Bass said as if prompted. "We'd all feel better if you had a good adviser. Listen, Ron, all hell is breaking loose here. We've had a lot of calls . . ."

"So have I . . ."

"The parents are frantic. What is the security situation there?"

"None of the female students are going out alone. Everyone's being careful. The police are very cooperative."

"I shouldn't have to tell you that we're all worried." Bass hesitated a moment before continuing. "There have been suggestions that you close down for this semester."

"That would be a mistake," Gregg said sharply. He restrained himself from telling Bass that a closedown would doom Willington's chances of ever opening again in Aix. "I don't expect further trouble," he said.

"Well, you're our man on the spot. We can only go by your guidance. Keep me informed, Ron."

"I will, Carlton."

"Good. I'll let you know about the lawyer. God bless."

"Good-bye."

Dr. Gregg sat still for a few moments. His administrative assistant was out of the office. For the first time, he found himself wishing he knew where she hid her gin bottle.

Marcia Chappel downed her first cognac at the zinc bar of Le Select and ordered another. It had stopped raining, robbing her of the excuse she'd found to duck into the café. The crowded bar was comfortable and she had no great desire to hurry back to the office. A few of the male customers had eyed her with appreciation as she'd entered, giving her the slow, ankle-to-head examination that seemed to be a Mediterranean specialty. Now, as the *patron* filled her glass with the amber brandy, she felt warm and more at ease than she'd been for weeks.

She really hadn't had time to examine her thoughts since Ginnie Feldman's death. The second murder had affected her even more. It wasn't that she'd been frightened, it just seemed that so much tragedy, so much bad luck, was unexplainable. If it hadn't been for her loyalty to Dr. Gregg, she'd have left by now. A New England Christmas would have been a good antidote to her depression, and she might even have been tempted to see Dr. Sichburn again. What would he have told her about her feelings for Dr. Gregg? He certainly wasn't a young man, so Sichburn's theory on the need for a son-lover wouldn't have been valid.

She lifted the small glass and sipped the cognac, appreciating its warmth as it slid down her throat. The barman had returned to the end of the counter to continue his conversation with a husky flower vendor in a black leather jacket. It took Marcia Chappel some time before she realized they were talking about her. She couldn't hear what they were saying. It was just as well.

"That," the vendor commented, "could be interesting."

"*Tu parles!*" the *patron* replied. "Have you developed a taste for lesbians?"

"Not at all. You're wrong. There's a very interesting body under that severe clothing. Seldom used, perhaps, but ripe."

"*Salaud!* Your wife looks like a film star compared to that foreigner."

The flower vendor shook his head. "You miss the point. My wife is my wife. But I sense a buildup of pressure in that woman. You can almost feel it."

An unexpected ray of sunshine played over the bottles behind the bar. Marcia Chappel forgot about the men and read the labels, a secret game she'd invented. Cinzano, Ricard, Cap Corse, Pernod, 51, Byrhh, Martell, Courvoisier, Hennessy, Fernet Branca, Old Lady's Gin, Johnny Walker, King's Ransom, Four Roses, Chartreuse, Izarra, Framboise. Each bottle a unique and independent entity with its distinctive colored label. She envisioned a large, framed collage of the labels as her souvenir of France. It somehow

seemed appropriate. She put aside her empty glass, left enough
money on the bar and nodded a good-bye to the *patron*.

"Au revoir, Mademoiselle," he called as the door shut behind
her. "There," he chided the flower vendor, "you've missed your
chance."

The vendor shrugged his shoulders. "On the contrary," he replied, "she's the loser."

It was still cold, but an intermittent sun played on the damp
façades of the old houses. Some residents had opened their shutters, hoping to catch a bit of natural warmth. Marcia Chappel felt
more able to face the office now. She knew that other students
would be leaving soon. She couldn't blame them . . . or their parents. One murder was more than enough. Two murders were a
gross exaggeration. Stepping over the puddles on the uneven cobblestones, she tried to guess what would happen next. The board of
regents and the president of Willington might well close down the
whole program. The French might decide they'd had enough and
ask them to leave. She sidestepped a large woman in a green wool
coat who was urging her dachshund to relieve himself on the narrow sidewalk.

If the Willington program was forced to leave Aix, there was no
doubt she'd have to find another job. Dr. Gregg, she reasoned with
a tinge of resentment, would be all right. He would resume his
teaching on the home campus and probably benefit from a certain
morbid celebrity status.

She didn't begrudge Gregg his position of tenure, but she
couldn't condone his cold attitude to the murders. She still felt
sorry for him. Pure bad luck, she thought, turning into a small
square. It was almost as if the whole Willington project had been
doomed from the start.

She paused, listening. Someone was singing by the small stone
fountain in the center of the square. The voice sounded familiar.
She knew the song. It was a Joan Baez hit of the '60s, the words
conjuring up a crowd of pushing, shoving demonstrators in front
of the Pentagon. They sounded strangely dated and out of place
echoing off the ancient stones of old Aix. She walked toward the
small group of listeners. The singer's an American, she told herself, no doubt about that.

The young man had one leg braced on the fountain's basin, his head was bent low over his guitar as if he were playing for himself. His open guitar case held several coins. A passing housewife added two more before continuing on her way. Marcia Chappel moved to a better vantage point. Unlike most street musicians, the singer had short-cropped blond hair and was neatly dressed. She chewed on her lower lip, trying to remember where she'd heard a voice like that before. It could have been anywhere on the Cours Mirabeau, where the singers congregated. She dug into her handbag, came up with three one-franc pieces and moved forward to drop them into the guitar case. The singer looked up to nod his thanks and returned her smile. Still singing, he watched her until she was out of sight. She remembered the other voice later. It had belonged to a young, scruffy type with long hair and a headband. It was surprising how two people could sound so alike.

"That's it," Mattei said gleefully, clapping his hands together. "It's got to be the young Boche."

"We'll need a hell of a lot more to find him," Bastide said doubtfully, shaking out his trench coat and hanging it on the rack near the door.

"I know," Mattei said, "but at least we've got the link between Magabian's employee and the Tholonet murder. It must be the same person."

Bastide put both hands in his trouser pockets and paced back and forth in front of his desk. "Now," he said, "we've got to find the bastard. Send Lenoir over to the German consulate to see how they keep track of their students in the Aix-Marseille region. Give them our best description. Have him ask about photo records, passports issued here and the troublemakers or psychos among their nationals. I stopped at a trailer camp three miles from the *cabanon*. The owner keeps his small shop open during the winter for the locals. He confirmed Magabian's description. The young *Chleub* used to buy bread and beer from him. He said he was quiet and polite."

"Don't any of the other residents remember him?" Mattei asked.

"Most of the houses are closed for the winter. A caretaker had seen smoke coming from the *cabanon*, but he didn't know who'd been in it."

"Who did you say owned the place?"

"A certain Antoine Grimaud . . . of Nice. The *Chleuh* was evidently a friend of his son. Young Grimaud is off in the mysterious east up to his ass in gurus and opium. Get Lenoir moving and call Nice. Have them dig the old man out of the woodwork. See what he can tell us. You better prepare a list of questions. Our colleagues over there are a bit slow . . . they eat too much polenta."

"Talking about food," Mattei said, "I'll buy you lunch."

"Bravo, Babar! It's not often I hear that. But we won't have much time."

"*Tant mieux.* I think what we need is a nice, inexpensive snack. A *pan bagnat* would do me fine."

Bastide chuckled. "I'm not letting you off that easy," he said. "You'll be glad to know that Aynard has decided I, too, need to lose weight. As soon as you get through to Nice I'll choose somewhere appropriate. In the meantime, I'll see if those composite drawings from Magabian's description are finished. We can start distributing them after lunch.

An hour later they were sitting at a plastic-topped table in the rear room of Chez Barone on the rue Vacon. They'd inspected Barone's sidewalk display of shellfish before entering the small restaurant. The open wooden cases and baskets were filled with fresh products of the sea packed in seaweed or bedded on chipped ice. There were black mussels from Bouzigues; glistening spiny sea urchins from the calanques southwest of Marseille; *palourdes, clovisses* and *praires,* of the clam family; and tiny, succulent *telines,* with blue-tinted shells, to be cooked with garlic, parsley and olive oil. Live spiny lobsters and crabs, their claws secured with raffia, bubbled and waved their antennae and legs beside the more dormant langoustines. The selection of oysters ranged from flat, meaty *belons* to craggy, deep-shelled *portugaises;* from tangy *vertes claires* to the new hybrids originating in Japan. Ugly *violets,* a Marseille favorite, lay in a tray like mud-covered roots and exuded the strong odor of iodine. Mounds of tiny gray shrimp were side by side with large Spanish *gambas* and red-shelled, cooked *crevettes.*

It hadn't taken Bastide and Mattei long to make up their minds. Now, with a bottle of the house white wine before them, they were waiting to be served.

"I should have known better," Mattei lamented. "Weight for weight, shellfish is the most expensive commodity on the market."

"Relax," Bastide replied, lifting his glass. "Where else can you get a good house wine at this price? Besides, Aynard would be proud of us. Shellfish are nonfattening . . . and they put lead in your pencil."

"That, I can do without," Mattei grumbled, "I'm already overloaded."

"*L'omelette aux oursins?*" the waiter asked, balancing his serving trays over their heads.

"For me," Mattei told him, smiling as the steaming, golden omelette with its filling of scarlet, tender sea urchins was put before him.

"*Et voilà,*" the waiter said, serving Bastide. "A dozen *portugaises* for Monsieur."

The opened oysters gleamed on their half shells, awash in their natural juices.

"Beautiful," Bastide commented, breathing deeply. "What an aroma. Nothing can match that."

"Three quarters nuclear waste," Mattei commented, his mouth full of omelette, "one quarter coastal sewage."

"Don't be bitter, Babar," Bastide laughed. "I could have chosen a lobster."

"What do you really think?" Mattei asked, suddenly serious.

"I think these *portugaises* are delicious."

"No, no. I mean the suspect. Do you really think he's our man?"

Bastide squeezed lemon juice over one of his oysters, watching them contract. "Babar, you know I don't believe in mixing business with eating. But, as you're paying the bill, the answer is yes. I believe he *is* our man."

Bastide cut an oyster from its shell with the edge of his small fork and slid it into his mouth, tasting its delicate, briny flavor. He swallowed it and began to butter a slice of brown bread.

"There is one thing that bothers me," Bastide said.

"What's that," Mattei asked.

"He's bound to hit again. His kind always do."

"If that's the case," Mattei said, "we shouldn't be sitting here."

Bastide smiled. "At the rate you're demolishing that omelette, we won't be here long."

Fred Feldman waited in the high-ceilinged, marble-floored reception area of the American embassy under the watchful eye of a black Marine Corps sergeant manning a checkpoint just inside the door. Feldman had an appointment with the embassy security officer, and he was waiting for a secretary to guide him to his office. An old college friend had arranged the meeting after Feldman had found that his contact in the embassy had been transferred to Moscow. Feldman took off his damp Burberry. He'd walked to the embassy from the Hôtel Prince de Galles and a sudden rainstorm had caught him on the Champs Élysées. He glanced at his watch. They'd already kept him waiting for ten minutes.

High heels clicking on the marble alerted him to the secretary's approach. She introduced herself and led the way upstairs past rattling teletype machines and busy offices.

The security officer's name was O'Brien. He reminded Feldman of a New York detective, but he was well dressed. He had red hair and a red face and talked as if his State Department service had smoothed some rough edges.

"Mr. Feldman," O'Brien said when Feldman was seated comfortably in an imitation-leather armchair. "I had a call from our mutual friend, Art Leeson, and I've been expecting you. What can I do to help?"

Telephones were ringing in the outer office and Feldman sensed that O'Brien would be glad to finish their business quickly. "Mr. O'Brien," Feldman said, "my daughter was murdered in Aix."

O'Brien tapped a tan folder lying on his desk. "I've been reviewing the background. I'm very sorry."

"Yes, well . . . now there's been a second murder."

O'Brien nodded. "I know," he said. "We're in touch with our consulate in Marseille. They're keeping us informed on both murders."

"That's just fine, but can't we do something about the French police?"

"Do something?"

"Light a fire under them! Get them moving!"

"I understand your position. It's frustrating for all of us. But we can't do much more than wait at this point. We are making sure they understand how concerned we are."

"You don't have anyone down in Marseille?"

"Not from this office."

"Oh, for Christ's sake! You're supposed to protect Americans, aren't you?"

"Mr. Feldman, let me explain. We *are* in France. They have their own methods. All we can do is offer help if they need it. I'm not running a criminal task force or an investigative bureau. Our job is embassy security, and believe me, it's a full-time job. But we are in touch with the French police constantly, and the murder of two young Americans is of great concern to us."

"How about private investigators?" Feldman asked, containing his anger. "Could you recommend one?"

"I wouldn't recommend using a private investigator in France."

"Why not?"

"It's not the same. You won't find a Sam Spade here. Their investigators are useful in divorce cases, property disputes, digging in archives. You seldom find them involved in murders. There's another drawback. The police don't like them."

"What else is new?" Feldman asked.

"Seriously, I wouldn't touch one if I were you."

"So, I sit and wait?"

"I really don't know what to tell you. If you're planning to stay in Marseille or Aix for some time, I'm sure the police would agree to keep you informed on a priority basis. They're good about such things."

"Such things? I would hope so! Do you realize how many times my girl was stabbed? You probably don't. I do." Feldman was on the edge of his chair, the veins building in his neck, his eyes hard and his hands shaking. "I hear the same thing happened to her roommate. Jesus, you'd think they'd have been able to save that poor kid. But no, they let her go around unescorted. What the hell kind of a police operation is that?"

O'Brien's secretary opened the door. "Excuse me, Mr. O'Brien," she said, eyeing Feldman with disapproval, "I wanted to remind you of the ambassador's staff meeting."

O'Brien checked the time quickly. "Thanks, Doreen," he said. "I didn't know it was so late. Mr. Feldman, how long are you going to be in Paris?"

"I'm leaving for Marseille tomorrow morning."

"I'll have a list of a few Marseille police officials delivered to your hotel this afternoon. You can use my name in contacting them. I hope they'll be able to help. Now, I apologize but I've got this meeting . . ." He extended his hand.

"Thanks," Feldman replied, rising from his chair. As they shook hands Feldman spoke confidentially.

"Listen, O'Brien," he said softly, "this is between us, but I have a question."

"Shoot," O'Brien said, waiting.

"How do I go about getting a handgun permit here?"

"Oh, you don't want to do that," O'Brien replied, shaking his head. "First of all, they'd never grant it to you. Secondly, there's no reason for it."

"I've got two at home."

"That's different."

"How different? I'm not snooping into a murder at home. My girl was killed by some maniac in Aix. I've got the right to protect myself."

"Mr. Feldman," O'Brien told him in his official voice, "I strongly advise you against buying or procuring an arm in this country."

Feldman took a deep breath, his eyes still on O'Brien's florid face. "Very well," he said, "thanks for your time."

"Say hello to Art when you see him," O'Brien called before Feldman was out of sight.

"Bad news," O'Brien murmured, writing something on a yellow ruled pad before hurrying to the staff meeting.

The last time Mattei had visited the Café des Colonies, someone had slashed his tires. Now, as he pulled up, he drove onto the sidewalk and parked just in front of the door, where he could keep an eye on his Mercedes. He hadn't been back to the café much since his informer Jo Jo le Lièvre had had his throat slit in Le Panier, but it was still the hangout of a rich cross section of the

Marseille underworld. It was the type of dive that had to be read
like a litmus paper. The customers, their presences or absences,
their reactions, their moods and the mood of the *patron* had to be
observed and judged for clues to what was going on in the streets.

The *patron* was already complaining as Mattei pushed open the
cracked door. "*Alors?* You can't find another place to park? You're
blocking my door!"

"*Ta gueule!*" Mattei growled, shaking the rain from his wool cap
and hanging it on a radiator beside the bar. "*Bonjour, tout le monde!*"
he greeted the customers. They included Bouche d'Or the pimp
and Georges d'Astier, a specialist in stripping gullible tourists of
their traveler's checks and passports. Ramon Souche the racetrack
tout was absent, but there were two other men drinking coffee at
the bar. He'd never seen them before. Either they were good at cop
sniffing or the *patron* had made some cautionary comment as Mattei walked in. The two had quickly turned their backs and were
apparently in deep conversation. Mattei surveyed the café. The
murals of the South Sea Islands were slowly fading under a greasy
patina of thick dust.

Mattei leaned on the bar, unperturbed at not having his cheerful
greeting returned. "A hot grog," he ordered, "and try putting
some rum in it for a change."

He turned and surveyed the strangers. He noted the Italian
shoes, the well-cut suits and the cuffs on the clean shirts. One of
them was wearing a gray felt hat. The other had thick black hair
styled with a razor cut. They weren't the type who usually fre-
quented the Café des Colonies. Mattei was intrigued.

The *patron* put the steaming grog on the bar, and Mattei tapped
his thick, hairy arm. "Who're your new playmates?"

His query produced a detached shrug. "I don't know."

"Then, I'll have to find out."

Mattei lifted his grog and took a quick sip. He unbuttoned his
jacket, his right hand surreptitiously freeing the holster snap of the
Colt on his right hip, and moved quickly to the other end of the
bar. He turned and faced the two men.

"Messieurs," he said, feigning a broad smile, "I'd like you to
settle a little argument. The *patron* says you're from Toulon. I say

you're from Nice. It's sort of a game we play here. Who is correct?"

The man with the hat had the face of an overdried prune. A thin mustache etched his upper lip like a frayed piece of gray string. His eyes were deep-set and coal black. The shorter man, with the Travolta haircut, had the same eyes. He was much younger. Gray scar tissue ran from the corner of his mouth to his right ear.

"Neither of you," the older man replied coldly. "We're in business . . . in Lyon."

From his new vantage point, Mattei could see the silk ties and the wide lapels of their jackets. He'd also caught the unmistakable trace of a Nice accent.

"Lyon? I could have sworn you were from Nice. If you had been, I'd have asked you about my old friend Bartolomei Grondona, alias 'Le Loup.' " The mention of the Niçois gang chief brought a quick flicker of concern from the young man. The older man's eyes remained flat and unexpressive.

"Well," Mattei remarked, "I've made a mistake."

He went back to his grog and winked at the *patron*. The *patron* ignored him. "Now," Mattei said loudly, "down to business." He reached into his inner pocket and produced a sheaf of papers. They were composite drawings by a police artist based on descriptions of the murder suspect.

"Here we are," Mattei said, smoothing out the sheets. "There's enough for everyone." He moved down the bar, putting a drawing in front of Bouche d'Or and Georges d'Astier.

"This is the drawing of a murder suspect. It's the best we have to go on for the moment. The murders took place in the Aix region, but the suspect worked in Marseille."

The *patron* dried his hands, examined the drawing and spun it back onto the bar. "We don't get that kind in here," he said.

"I know you don't," Mattei replied with exaggerated patience, "but your customers get around. All I ask is that they keep their eyes and ears open. This nice young man murdered two American girls." Mattei turned quickly toward Bouche d'Or. "*Eh, ami,*" he said, "you don't have daughters but you run a lot of girls. They're all the family you've got. You wouldn't like any of them murdered, would you?"

Bouche d'Or grunted, buried his face in his glass of rosé and moved away from Mattei.

"This suspect," he told everyone, "is a German; his long hair is blond and he stabs his victims with an ice pick."

Mattei finished the last of his grog. "I'll leave a few here. You can hand them out to your clients at apéritif time. He picked up his cap from the radiator and put it on. He dropped a few drawings in front of the two strangers.

"Here," he said, "take them back with you . . . to Nice. Who knows? It's a small world."

Dinh Le Thong examined the drawing carefully, scratched his head and removed the ivory toothpick from his mouth.

"Not very distinctive," he commented.

Bastide drew on his cigar and blew a smoke ring toward the low ceiling of Le Haiphong. "Add a German accent, paint the eyes blue and the hair blond," he said. "It's not much, but it's the best we've got."

The waitress Thong claimed as a niece was scrubbing the tile floor on her hands and knees. A steady chopping echoed from the kitchen, and two small Vietnamese children were laboriously placing bottles of beer in the frigidaire behind the bar. An old Charles Trenet record was playing softly in the background.

"A cognac?" Thong asked.

"*Non, merci.* It's too early. I've got to take a quick swim at the club and get back to the office to see what Lenoir's come up with at the German consulate. They might be able to help. I think I'll try Interpol. You can never tell."

Thong made a disparaging gesture. "Interpol is about as useful as UNESCO in matters of this kind." He studied the drawing once more, frowning.

"If he cut his hair," Thong continued, "it would make this drawing useless. You know your average *flic* or *gendarme*. He looks at a photo or drawing of someone with long hair . . . he's got to find someone with long hair."

Bastide agreed. He buttoned his coat and they shook hands.

Thong walked him to the door. "You're in a strange business, Roger. Don't you ever get sick of it?"

"Oh, there are moments. But what else can I do? If I were a chef, like you, I might take early retirement."

"But you are a good cook."

"Let's be serious. I do well enough in my small kitchen, un-rushed and with a few friends to feed. I'd be a disaster trying to please a restaurant full of clients."

"But you still enjoy police work?"

Bastide paused to consider Thong's question. "It's not so much that I enjoy it. It's my profession. That doesn't tell you much, but it sums up why I stick with it."

"I know what you mean. I think of the old days occasionally. You were too young for Indochina. It was very special. The morning mists moving through the valleys near Lao Cai, the call of the jungle birds, the deadly quiet as our ambush parties watched the Viet rafts float toward us on the dark surface of the Red River. It was a different world. It was my country."

"*Allez*, Thong." Bastide grasped his friend's arm. "Don't go sentimental on me. You still manage to keep your hand in," he said, referring to Thong's unofficial work for the Direction Générale de la Sécurité Extérieure.

"You know all the dark secrets of my life." Thong grinned. "*Bonne chasse!*"

Bastide drove through the heavy afternoon traffic to the Cercle Sportif. It had stopped raining by the time he got there. He went to his locker, changed into his trunks and took a lukewarm shower before going to the heated indoor pool. There were only a few other swimmers, all males, splashing through their laps in the echoing, glass-domed interior. He plunged into the water with a shallow, racing dive and managed three lengths before his pounding heart and a lightness in his legs told him it was time to stop. His eyes burned from the chlorine and his arms were stiff as he climbed up a metal ladder and began to dry himself.

He sat on a bench, the towel over his shoulder, and thought about Thong's question: "You still enjoy police work?" Had he enjoyed it at the beginning? He must have. It had been a natural progression when he'd left the Army after Algeria. Perhaps "enjoy" wasn't the right word. He hadn't had much time to think lately. Now, as he shut his eyes and tried to be honest with himself,

he found it difficult. Someone had once suggested that he transfer
to another section. A year or two in Narcotics or Antigang might
change his perspective and break the routine he'd become used to
in Homicide. Despite its depressing aspects, he still found Homicide fascinating. It represented the knife's edge of human relations.
A very special domain open only to a few who had the question-
able privilege of dealing with the dark side of reality. Thong had
wished him good hunting. That might be part of it. To hunt and
find a murderer gave him a certain undefined pleasure that he'd
never mentioned to anyone. It was too private, too personal.

He glanced up at the large clock above the starting blocks. It was
time to go. As he walked to the showers again, he wondered if
Mattei had ever been asked the same question. He toyed with the
idea of asking Mattei but decided against it. Things were fine as
they were. No use turning his office into a psychiatric clinic.

CHAPTER VII

The first day of December was flint gray, and there was the threat of snow in the air. White smoke coughed from automobile exhausts as drivers urged their reluctant motors into action and moved slowly over the slippery cobblestones. The municipal workers of Aix had begun to install holiday decorations along the Cours Mirabeau. Licorice-like coils of insulated wire blocked sections of the sidewalk as electricians spliced the connections that would soon turn the bare tree branches into a luminous fairyland. A wandering artist had already decorated the windows and bar mirrors of some cafés with Christmas scenes in chalky reds and greens. Père Noël surrounded by holly and red berries, popping champagne corks, bubble-filled glasses and snow-capped fir trees were the extent of his repertoire. He'd also lettered the mirrors with the holiday menus, listing courses, wines and the all-inclusive prices.

The smart shops were bright with color and rich with quality products. The *charcuteries* were announcing the provenance and prices of their *foie gras* and caviar. Butchers were hanging displays of game and game birds from their racks and canopies: russet-haired wild boar, hare, multicolored wild ducks, small deer, long-tailed pheasant and needle-beaked woodcock and snipe dripped blood onto the dry sawdust. Deep plates of rich terrines and mounds of plump *boudin blanc* sausages decorated with Christmas greenery filled the display windows. There was a palpable change in the air. People moved quicker. They were more apt to smile. The end of the month promised relaxation, *gourmandise* and a new beginning.

The minstrel propped his guitar against the stone wall and wrapped a wool scarf more tightly around his throat. He retrieved some coins from the open guitar case and dropped them into his pocket. He'd found a sheltered spot not far from the Palais de

Justice. One hour of performing had already provided him with enough for dinner.

He was pleased with his new image. Since he'd been back in Aix, he'd cultivated his role as an American. He'd sought out his fellow countrymen, easily identifiable in the cafés and along the Cours Mirabeau by their accents. He'd introduced himself as Buddy Warren, thinking it a good joke to adopt the detested label his stepfather had given him. His knowledge of Aix had helped in making contacts. He knew the cheapest restaurants, the liveliest bars, the small, off-beat hotels. His new friends were fascinated by the handsome American who actually supported himself as a street singer. His accent often puzzled them, but he explained that he'd been brought up in Germany, where his father had been a colonel in the American Army.

He'd also made a discovery. The change in his appearance had made it easier to earn money. He'd been astounded at the number of people who'd stopped to drop coins in the case of a short-haired, neatly dressed singer. They were the same people who had hurried past him, eyes averted, when he'd performed long-haired and unwashed in the same location. He'd even received a smile and a nod of greeting from a passing policeman.

Buddy Warren, a.k.a. Otto Rupert Warren, picked up his guitar and began to strum an introduction to his country-and-western repertoire. He was comparatively happy. He was eating well and he could afford a bath once a week. The Americans he'd met were generous with their grass and hashish. He'd introduced them to some dealers and picked up a bonus for it in the form of quality coke. Things were looking up. He shut his eyes and began to sing about a whining whistle in the West Virginia hills, smoky valleys and a "li'l blond gal." The description reminded him of the girl he'd left in the cave. His recollections were vague in detail and detached . . . part of another life. They flickered on the edge of his consciousness. When he'd finished the song, on a long high note, and opened his eyes, he'd garnered a few new coins. A small boy was being urged forward by his mother, a fifty-centime piece extended in his pudgy hand.

"Come feed the monkey," the minstrel murmured.

The boy dropped the coin and rushed back to the protection of his mother's skirt. The minstrel bowed elaborately and launched into a ballad. Now he thought about the other American, the older woman, the one who smiled and always gave him a few francs. He knew she was an American, because he'd heard her talking one day on the terrace of Le Grillon. The specter of the blonde faded from his mind as he concentrated on his new preoccupation. She must be about the same age as his mother. He wondered if she was a whore too. She didn't wear much makeup, but that didn't fool him. She was probably as bad as the others. He imagined her stripped of her conservative suit, standing in her underwear, her arms outstretched to a man. He wondered how she would have liked his stepfather and what he used to do to his mother. She'd like it, he told himself, she'd love it, writhing and groaning under the weight of that thick-necked bastard!

"Hey, Buddy!" A tall American student with a fuzzy beard was calling to him. "Buy you a coffee?"

The minstrel nodded, ended his song abruptly with a final strum and began to gather the coins.

"You always look so grim when you're singing?" the American asked.

"Shit, no, man," the minstrel replied. "It's just indigestion."

What other school administrator had ever been under such pressure? Dr. Gregg asked himself the question but already knew the answer. He was the sole recipient of the dubious honor. His day had begun with a long-distance conversation with the parents of Jean Bates. There had been the unspoken implication that he was somehow responsible for their daughter's death. He had been able to tell them the arrival time of the coffin containing the girl's body and assured them that Willington would cover the costs of embalming and shipment.

Then Hank Castel had informed him that Fred Feldman was back in Aix. This was particularly upsetting to Gregg. He knew Feldman didn't like him. He had the uneasy feeling that Ginnie's father was a form of unguided missile. He was suspicious of the obvious link between Mr. Feldman and Hank Castel. He would have to gain Feldman's confidence, but he didn't know how to go about it.

Earlier, he had gone through the ordeal of saying good-bye to Professor Costin. It had been awkward. The storklike Costin had sat slumped in a chair, his bald head lowered, while Gregg expressed his sorrow at the course of events that had made the professor's resignation a necessity. When he'd handed Costin a carefully worded letter covering his work at Willington prior to the Feldman murder, Costin had snatched it without a word and stuffed it into a trouser pocket. Marcia Chappel had already paid Costin his wages as well as a small refund for his health insurance. When Gregg had finished his words of regret and waited for Costin's response, there had been an interminable silence. Then Costin had raised his head, glared at Gregg and responded with one word: "Fascist!" Gregg had never been called *that* before. By the time he'd recovered from the shock, Costin was gone for good.

Now another trial lay ahead of him. He would have to see Madame de Rozier. She had arbitrarily withdrawn a young teacher of French from the Willington program on the excuse that the university itself needed her services. This was patently untrue. Gregg wondered if it was only the beginning of a freezing-out process. He'd debated with himself the best way to deal with Madame de Rozier. He had come to the reluctant conclusion that he'd call on her in her office. Harley Cannon's lawyer friend was due to arrive in two days. He had to smooth the old hen's ruffled feathers. Gregg knew anyone recommended by Cannon would also be reported to President Carlton. He knew Madame de Rozier would like nothing better than to bypass him and find a direct channel for her complaints to Willington. He'd have to swallow what pride he had left, smile and butter up the old bitch.

He took off his spectacles and spun them idly in one hand, frowning. The lawyer was going to be a problem. He didn't know what he was going to do with him. Willington did have a local *notaire* working for them on a contract basis to handle minor legal matters. He decided to stick the *notaire* with Cannon's friend, have him introduced to the law faculty and the police and ensure some good, heavy lunches with his French colleagues in Marseille. That should keep him out from underfoot for a while.

Craig ran a hand through his short-cropped hair. What did it all have to do with education? Not a goddamn thing. He hadn't really thought about education or learning in the past few days. He'd been concentrating on administration and murder. It was a bizarre situation. Somewhere out there, beyond the confines of his high-ceilinged, drafty office, was a killer who had murdered two of his students. He pondered the killer's choice. Why Willington? God knows. Aix was crawling with students of every nationality, including those from the other American institutes. What strange quirk of the mind, Gregg asked himself with a touch of self-pity, what perverted sense of logic, aimed the killer at Willington's students?

Lenoir came back from the German consulate empty-handed. He'd been received with cool courtesy and allowed a behind-the-scenes look at Teutonic efficiency. A young male consul with corn-silk hair had asked a number of questions, studied the composite drawing carefully, pored rapidly over some modern filing cabinets and tapped at a small computer. After a brief phone call, he'd locked his cabinets and left Lenoir alone for ten minutes. When he'd returned, he had a short printout and several passport renewal forms complete with photographs of the applicants. Most had renewed their passports over a year before in Marseille while traveling. None of them bore the slightest resemblance to the composite drawing. Regardless, the consul had given Lenoir a copy of the list, pointing out the home addresses of the applicants and offering further assistance if needed. By the time he returned to the hôtel de police, it was dark. The overhead light in Bastide's office still hadn't been replaced. Its flickering gave the room the luminosity of a silent movie. Bastide was on the telephone to Aix. Lenoir sat at Mattei's desk to wait. Bastide put down the receiver. He glanced at Lenoir and lit a stubby Havana, playing the match flame over its tip and drawing on it slowly.

"That was Guignon," he told Lenoir. "He's bitching again. He's picked up enough German students to form an SS division and he's worried about legal problems. He says none of them look like probables. One won't stop crying and another threw up on his rug. How about you?"

Lenoir described his visit to the German consulate and produced the list. Bastide was unimpressed. He pushed the list aside and

leaned back in his chair, both hands behind his head. He was thinking of something Thong had said. "If he cut his hair, it would make
this drawing useless." He sat up straight. "The wisdom of the mysterious East," he remarked.

"What's that?" Lenoir asked.

"Get hold of that artist," Bastide told him. "I want him to re-
work the drawing. I want a short-haired suspect."

"But the German had long hair."

"*Eh bien*, lard-head! You're confirming Thong's theory!"

"I don't get it."

"You wouldn't. Now get moving!"

Lenoir checked his watch. "The artist's gone home by now," he
said, hesitating.

Bastide stood up, bringing Lenoir to his feet. He pushed an in-
dex finger into Lenoir's chest. "You go to the artist's house. You
grab him by the ear. You bring him back here. You sit him down
and see that he draws what we want. You bring the results to me at
my apartment. Understood?"

"Yes, sir."

"Good. Now *grouille!*"

Janine Bourdet sat in Bastide's kitchen sipping a dry vermouth
and watching him slice a *saucisson d'Arles*. She was dressed for a
night out, in an oyster-white Chanel-Lagerfeld suit. He handed her
a thin piece of *saucisson* and turned back to his stove. He was wearing an old pair of jeans, wool sweater and espadrilles. The cannelloni shells were cooking gently. The filling for them, a blend of
finely chopped veal, raw ham and onion moistened with a glass of
white wine and flavored with a touch of thyme and bay leaf, was
reducing in a covered skillet.

"So you won't go with me to the Opéra?" Janine asked.

Bastide stopped slicing the *saucisson*, checked the spinach he'd
cleaned earlier and turned toward her.

"The answer is no."

"It's nothing modern or esoteric. It's Carmen."

He drank from a glass of pastis and wiped his other hand on his
butcher's apron. "I can't go tonight. Lenoir's coming on business."

She grimaced. "You wouldn't come anyway. Does culture bother you?"

He sighed and returned to his cooking. "Culture does *not* bother me," he replied. "I admit I'm not an intellectual, but I have nothing against culture."

"Bravo, Monsieur l'Inspecteur," she chided him. "I'll sleep better now, knowing the police position on the arts."

"Call up old Gautier," Bastide countered, lifting the cover off the cannelloni stuffing and poking at it with a wooden spoon. "I'm sure he'd be glad to sleep through a performance beside you."

He put down the spoon and walked over to Janine. He crouched beside her chair and took her chin in his hand.

"What's the problem?" he demanded. "It's more than the *sacré* opera. You're in a bad mood tonight."

She turned away, looking toward the window.

"Maybe it's the weather," she said. "When it rains like this, I get *le cafard.*"

Bastide stood up, smiling. "*Bon sang!*" he said, "let's not ruin the dinner. These cannelloni will cheer you up. It's my mother's recipe . . . good for miserable weather. You'll feel better when we eat."

"You're probably right," she said, taking a bite of the *saucisson.* "I don't want to go to the opera either."

He put the spinach into a covered pot. It would quickly steam in its own juice. "Good. Now we can relax."

She went to the window to stare at the wet streets and the dark water of the Vieux Port. He observed her in silence, appreciating the proportions of her generous figure and the sweep of her tanned legs. If Lenoir weren't coming by, he'd have proposed making love immediately, despite the ingredients simmering on the stove. But, knowing Lenoir, the idiot would undoubtedly appear at exactly the wrong moment. He concentrated on removing the pasta shells from the water without damaging them. He moved to the sink to rinse them with cold water. He laid them carefully on a clean dish towel to dry. Now all he had to do was add the spinach and some egg yolk to his stuffing, roll it in the cannelloni shells, put them in a baking dish bathed in Dominique's *sauce coulis,* cover them with melted butter and grated cheese and let the oven do the rest.

"Roger," Janine said softly, "I'm worried."

"About what?"

"Us."

He put his spoon down and put his arms around her waist. "What about us?" he asked, making an effort to sound receptive, but uneasy with the direction the conversation was taking.

"This can't go on forever," she said. "We've got to be realistic."

"We are."

"I don't think so. I've thought about it lately. Anything could happen. You could find someone else—"

"Don't be stupid!"

"Monsieur Gautier won't be around much longer. Have you thought of that?"

"Well, I—"

"You haven't, have you? What would happen to me? I've no other income. I'd have to leave Marseille. Or would you want me to find another *protecteur?*"

"Janine, what's got into you?"

"Oh, I know. I'm your kind of woman. I'm self-reliant, worldly, cynical. I'm excellent in bed . . . or in the kitchen or anywhere you want to take me. But I'm not sure it's enough."

"What the hell is that supposed to mean?" He was upset now. He left her and began rolling the cannelloni. *"Bonne mère!"* he thought, she had to catch me in the middle of cooking to begin a serious conversation. She'll be talking about marriage next.

"It's supposed to mean," she said, ". . . it does mean that we should try to think about the future."

"Damn!" he cursed. "Now you've made me rip a cannellone."

He was wiping some stuffing from his fingers when the doorbell buzzed. "Who is it?" he shouted angrily.

"Lenoir."

He released the double bolt to let the detective in. Lenoir's coat was black with dampness and he was drying his hair with a handkerchief. His blond mustache was drooping more than usual. He reached into an inner pocket and produced a brown envelope.

"The new *portrait-robot,"* he announced dramatically.

Bastide opened the envelope and examined the sketch. The artist had done a good job, retaining the bone structure and facial contours without destroying the basic likeness, but the short hair did change the appearance. If one had not seen the original, one might think it was an altogether different person.

"Not bad," Bastide said. "Now, I want copies for tomorrow. The same number as the original. Can you do that?"

"Yes, no problem."

Bastide smiled. "No problem! Who are you kidding? Those clowns in the printshop drag in about 10 A.M. Don't bother them tonight. But call the foreman at home about six in the morning. Tell him it's an emergency and we need the copies by eight. Tell him it's a special job for Commissaire Aynard."

"Consider it done."

"Good. Now, would you like a drink?"

"A drink?"

"Yes, Lenoir, a drink."

"Oh, thanks, but I don't have time. I've a rendezvous."

"Well, good night, then, and thank you."

Bastide bolted the door and walked back to the kitchen. Janine had refilled her glass and was waiting for him, leaning against the sink. Her large eyes were moist with tears, but she was smiling.

"I've repaired your cannellone," she told him.

He inspected it, nodding his approval.

"You know, Roger," she said, "you really missed your calling."

"How's that? You think I should have been a chef instead of a *poulardin?*"

"Oh no," she laughed, shaking her head, "with your sympathy and understanding of women, you would have made a first-class *maquereau.*"

The baking dish of cannelloni came out of the oven crusted and moist, the rich, bubbling sauce thoroughly blended with the butter and cheese. Janine had made a simple salad of *frisé* lettuce with sauce vinaigrette; Bastide brought a bottle of Bardolino and two clean glasses to the table. He filled the glasses as Janine spooned the cannelloni onto their warm plates. Bastide watched her with deep pleasure. She was beautiful, sensual and alive. He realized how fortunate he was to have her. As they touched glasses, the thought crossed his mind that perhaps he should be thinking more of their future.

Hank Castel met Fred Feldman in the bar of his hotel. Ginnie's father was on his second martini and he was obviously tense. He ordered a beer for Castel and launched into a description of his visit to the American embassy.

"So this so-called 'security' officer gave me a few minutes of his time," he related, "and told me zilch! It makes you wonder. What do we pay taxes for? He gave me the names of some French cops. Big deal! I could have managed that on my own." Feldman paused to down half of his drink. He pulled the olive from its toothpick and popped it into his mouth, chewing furiously. He looked at Castel for a moment without speaking.

"So," he finally asked, "what's new here?"

Castel poured some beer into his glass and shrugged his shoulders. "Not much," he said. "All I know is that the Willington program is in trouble. A lot of students have pulled out—"

"But what about the case? Have the cops got any leads?"

"If they do, they're not telling me. They did have a suspect. One of the professors. But that didn't work out."

"Why not?"

"The second murder took place while he was in custody."

"They think both murders were committed by the same person?"

"It looks that way."

Mr. Feldman slumped in his chair, staring at his glass and moving it in damp circles on the tablecloth. The bar was empty. They were the only customers, and the barman began mixing another martini the minute Feldman made a sign in his direction.

"I did get in touch with the Bateses," Feldman said. "Poor people! That girl was their whole life. The mother's crawled into her shell since the murder. The husband said she wouldn't even talk to their minister."

"How is Mrs. Feldman?" Hank ventured, feeling increasingly uneasy.

"She's coping, but that's about all."

The barman brought the third martini to their table. "This is Roland," Feldman said, introducing the barman. "He makes the best damn martinis in France. Where did you learn?"

"At the Negresco in Nice, monsieur," Roland responded with that strange blend of obsequiousness and superiority only French barmen can master.

"Hank," Feldman continued, "I did appreciate your calls." He sucked at his full glass and fumbled in his inner pocket. "Here," he said, "this is for you."

The check was for $300. Hank Castel began to protest. "I can't take this. The phone calls didn't cost that much."

"Take it. You earned it. Without you, I wouldn't have had a clue about what was going on."

Castel folded the check carefully and put it in his wallet. "What do you plan to do now?" he asked Feldman.

"First I'll see those police officials. Talk to the guys on the embassy list. But I don't have much hope. Then I'll get in touch with that detective . . . what's his name?"

"Mattei?"

"No, his boss."

"Inspecteur Bastide?"

"That's him. He looks like a reasonable character. At least he's actually on the case. With a little stroking, he might be helpful."

Castel was puzzled. What was Feldman after? The investigation would go along at its own momentum and his efforts certainly wouldn't help. Castel guessed Feldman only wanted to be a part of it. He was probably searching for some kind of psychological catharsis. He watched Feldman take another gulp of his martini. The poor bastard must be carrying a load of guilt around with him.

"How's my friend Dr. Gregg?" Feldman asked.

"He's under the gun. The university has sent a lawyer to help him, but there's a rumor that the French may ask Gregg to close down the Willington program."

"Serve the bastard right!"

"I think you're being unfair."

"Unfair? You're joking. I know his type. He thinks he's a latter-day Mr. Chips. Listen, I knew some of them when I was at Columbia. T.P.B., that's what I called them . . . tweeds, pipes and bullshit!"

"I think you're wrong. Gregg isn't my favorite, but he's doing his best. Personally I'd hate to see the Willington program ended."

Feldman glowered at him. Castel recognized the symptoms. The martinis were having their effect.

"Listen, Kid," Feldman told him with a humorless smile, "I'll be lucky to get out of here without knocking your Dr. Gregg flat on his ass."

She couldn't sleep. The streets were comparatively quiet, but disco music from the nearby cellar nightclub was sending its throbbing beat through the old stones of her apartment. She rolled over to look at the luminous dial of her bedside clock. It was past two. She fell back again, eyes open, and debated the pros and cons of taking a Valium tablet. She decided against it. It would guarantee a morning headache.

Marcia Chappel felt very lonely. She'd eaten by herself earlier at a cheap, self-service restaurant. The greasy *saucisse de Toulouse*, buried in a mound of gray mashed potatoes, sat heavily on her stomach. She blinked in the darkness, toting up her intake of alcohol for the day. She'd had a gin and bitter lemon before lunch, a cognac after the meal and two gin and tonics before dinner. When she'd come back to her apartment after dinner, she'd had another touch of gin to help her sleep. She didn't count the wine she'd had with her meals.

Her mind moved through a number of thoughts and memories. She recalled her first visit to France as an impressionable twenty-year-old. The sights, sounds and odors had been so different. The smell of strong, cheap tobacco in the Métro; the early-morning gurgle of water in the gutters as the street sweepers gave Paris its daily cleanup; the brightly painted barges gliding under the bridges of the Seine. It had all been a wonderland then, a time of great adventure, a moment of special promise. She couldn't help but make a comparison with the day that had just ended. Was time always measured in a graduated arc, one side up and the other forever downward?

She wracked her mind to find a more recent positive image and recalled the bar of Le Select and the man in the black leather jacket. She'd been aware that he'd spoken about her with the barman, and she'd sensed his interest. Even while concentrating on her cognac, she'd known somehow that she was being appreciated as a woman. Perhaps appreciated wasn't the proper word. They'd probably been considering her as a simple object, something to be used and discarded.

She constructed a dreamlike fantasy of her own. She'd accepted a drink from the leather jacket. He'd been charming, virile and very French. They'd had a long lunch together with much wine. He'd caressed her leg under the table and she hadn't pushed his hand away. When they'd left the restaurant, he'd put his arm around her and insisted she come to his room for a coffee. She'd accepted, knowing what was to come. He'd been surprisingly tender and considerate. He'd pulled the heavy drapes over the window and undressed her slowly, marveling at the promise of the body he was freeing from its camouflage of frilly blouse and tailored woolens.

Marcia Chappel rolled on her side, her fantasy gathering strength and substance. Her limited experience encouraged imaginative scenes of intense eroticism. Fondling herself, lips parted, eyes closed, she saw what happened in leather jacket's room through a clear lens. It thrilled and frightened her. She lifted her taut, full breasts for his kisses. She sought all he had to give with lustful determination. She moved jerkily in her own bed, making small catlike sounds. Moaning, she finally subsided, face down on her pillow. The sobs came then, spaced like deep hiccups, and she finally dropped off to sleep.

Claude Renucci was patrolling the Cours Mirabeau on foot. He'd joined the police two years previously and liked being in uniform. He was a short man. There had been some trouble about that, but one of his cousins had used his influence. That, and an extra inch added to his heels, had done the trick. He was an Aixois and he was perfectly content to serve in his own city. It was cold, and the unprotected café terraces were closed. The few people hurrying along the sidewalk were eager to reach their destinations. It looked like a dull afternoon. He was keeping his eye out for a team of young *tireurs* who'd been operating along the Cours in the past twenty-four hours. Their pickpocket technique was a variation of the bump routine with a new refinement. One of them, with a soft-drink cup in his hand, walked into an unsuspecting citizen and spilled the drink over his clothing. While the instigator offered his apologies, a second member of the team arrived to help the victim out of his jacket and dab at the stain with his handkerchief. The wallet was removed in the confusion. The third member of the team acted as a lookout during the operation. Their racket had been reported when a portly gentleman reached for his wallet to offer a tip to the solicitous young man who'd helped him dry his jacket, only to find his wallet missing.

Renucci had little hope of catching the trio. They'd probably moved on by now, and there weren't that many targets left on the street. He paused to gaze at a Mercedes convertible parked in front of a travel agency. Someday he'd have a car like that. An off-duty policeman waved to him from across the street and he returned the greeting. He walked on, passing the Grillon, watching the gray pigeons pecking at some spilled popcorn.

There were a group of young people ahead crowded around a bench. He examined them from a distance. All students . . . little chance of his pickpockets' being among them. As he drew closer, he could tell they were speaking in English. His brief attempt at the language in the *lycée* had at least provided that advantage. They were bundled in dull, padded jackets, colored wool caps and long scarves. He moved past them slowly, identifying the fragrance of hashish smoke. His eyes moved from face to face in what had now become an automatic, almost involuntary form of categorization.

Two years ago, the odor of hashish might have bothered him, even galvanized him into some form of action. Now it was different. One had to be realistic. Hashish was to heroin what beer was to eau de vie. The police could only do so much, and he'd worry about all that if he was ever assigned to Narcotics. He noted that one of the male students had a guitar case under his arm. A young brunette with granny glasses turned toward him and smiled. He touched his cap with two fingers in an informal salute and moved on.

Renucci reached the top of the Cours Mirabeau. He turned to retrace his steps and spotted a *nenette* coming out of the Hotel Dijon, wrapping the fur collar of her coat around her neck. At first he didn't recognize her, but she turned to glance in his direction and he saw it was Mado la Donneuse, a prostitute who often informed for the police. She walked in his direction, swinging her hips, a pout on her puffy lips.

"*Ciao*, Mado," he greeted her, nodding.

"*Tiens, tiens!*" she murmured in a gravelly voice. "Le Renuc is having his little walk."

"Yes, we have something in common . . . we both spend most of our time on the pavement."

She swept past him definitely, not deigning to reply.

Renucci began to laugh but stopped. A delayed mental reaction stopped him in his tracks. The blond kid with the guitar case! The *portrait-robot* on the bulletin board he'd seen that morning! He'd only glanced at it and he couldn't be sure, but there was enough of resemblance. He began to walk briskly down the Cours. The group of students had vanished. He looked up and down the street, checking both sidewalks. He examined the nearest side streets with no luck. Frustrated, he hurried back to the *poste de police* to examine the drawing.

He was reading the brief *note de service* under the portrait when a *sous-brigadier* came through the swinging doors from the inner office and saw him.

"Renucci!" the gray-haired sous-brigadier shouted, "what the hell are you doing here?"

"I'm checking this notice, *chef.*"

"I can see that. But you can wait till you're off duty to catch up on your reading. You're supposed to be patrolling the Cours." The sous-brigadier finally sensed Renucci's excitement. "Well?" he asked, "what's the problem?"

"I'm not sure, but I thought I just saw this type . . . with a group of students."

The sous-brigadier was suddenly interested. "Are you sure?" he asked, coming closer to read the notice himself.

"It looks like him. A blond. Either English or American."

"It says this one is German. He's on drugs and wanted for murder."

Renucci nodded, remembering the aroma of hashish.

"You didn't question him?"

"Well, I . . ."

"You really weren't sure?"

Not wanting to admit his delayed reaction, Renucci remained silent, frowning at the portrait.

"Listen, friend," the sous-brigadier told him, "one thing you've got to learn in this business is that most of these artists turn out pure crap. They distill a lot of wild imaginings into a monstrosity that we're supposed to recognize. If you were absolutely sure about this I'd give you a backup, ask for some plainclothes support and scour the Cours and the streets for your *blondiche*. So, are you sure or not?"

"It's difficult—"

"Get your tail back on patrol and don't let me see you in here until you're relieved! Understood?"

"*Oui, Chef,*" Renucci replied, backing out the door. He stopped to readjust his cap before returning to his beat. He was sure of one thing. If his suspicions ever proved correct, he'd make sure the sous-brigadier's nose was rubbed in it.

Bastide had been closeted with a judge for more than an hour, going over the evidence in an upcoming case. As he left the Palais de Justice, a timid sun had appeared over Marseille, limning vague shadows of the bare plane trees on the pavement. He hurried along the Cours Pierre Puget, glancing at his watch. He knew he could get a lift back to his office if he walked down to the Place de la Préfecture. All the new *portrait-robots* had been distributed and there might be some results or reactions by now. He paused, waiting for the traffic light on the rue de Breteuil and someone tapped his shoulder. He turned quickly, expecting a colleague, and found Mireille Peraud.

"Monsieur l'Inspecteur," she greeted him. "I've found you at last!"

They exchanged the ritual *bises*, a one-two-three cheek-kissing that engulfed him in her perfume and confirmed the softness of her skin.

"What are you doing?" he asked. "Shopping?"

"No, I've been at the Cercle for a meeting. I'm on one of those horrible committees trying to put together a schedule of activities for next year."

Mireille looked even more attractive, more feminine. Her blue eyes sparkled and her tawny hair escaped in thick waves from under a large tan beret. Her bulky tweed coat was cinched tight at the waist. Its thick material couldn't hide the fact that she had a very special figure.

"You haven't enough to do in Toulon?" Bastide asked.

"That's part of the problem, Roger. I'm still bored. Those navy wives . . ." She rolled her eyes and shook her head in mock despair.

"Which way are you going?" he asked, knowing the time was slipping by but not really wanting to leave.

"Down the rue Paradis to the Vieux Port."

"Good," he said, discarding his plan to walk to the Préfecture. "That's on my way. We can walk together."

He was slightly irritated. Each time he'd run into Mireille in the past year, it had been unplanned and unexpected. He'd never been prepared for their haphazard encounters or had time to think out his approach. Perhaps it was just as well. As she took his arm, he posed the usual questions about her husband. He was now in command of a destroyer on station near Beirut. There was always a surge of excitement when Bastide heard that Jacques Peraud was away. If ever there was to be something between them it would happen in Jacques's absence.

"You're on another case," Mireille said, watching him. "I can tell. You always have a troubled look. What is it this time?"

"Not much." He shrugged. "Two victims in Aix. Young American girls."

"Not much!" she remonstrated. "I've read about it. It sounds important to me . . . particularly for the poor girls."

"I didn't mean that," he told her, "but let's not talk police business. How long will Jacques be gone?"

"Aha!" she exclaimed, narrowing her eyes and feigning suspicion. "You've finally decided to take advantage of me. The poor wife wronged while her husband serves his country!" She looked up, prepared to laugh, but didn't. Bastide had paused. He was frowning. She moistened her lips with her tongue.

"It's not a joking matter?" she asked.

"It definitely is not," he replied seriously as they resumed walking.

She kept her head down for a long moment, thinking, before she glanced up at him again. "Perhaps we should talk about it?" she suggested.

"I don't think so," he said shortly.

"Please," she urged, pressing his arm. "I think it's important."

He sighed, feeling trapped, but led her into the nearest café. They sat at a formica table far from the bar. Bastide ordered two espressos. The *patron*'s dirty spaniel was sniffing among the cigarette butts and crumbs on the tile floor. The jukebox was blaring and two pinball machines were in play. He couldn't have picked a less romantic setting.

Mireille slipped out of her coat and hung it over the back of the chair. Her breasts strained against the white wool of her tight sweater. She cleared her throat and smiled. When their coffee was served, she sipped it, watching him over the rim of the cup.

"Mireille," he began, "this is ridiculous . . ."

"Do you really think so?"

"Yes."

"Then why," she asked, "is it 'no joking matter'?"

Bastide picked up his coffee, playing for time. A few minutes ago, he reflected, I was perfectly happy, doing my job with not too many complications. Suddenly I'm in serious discussion with a married woman about my desire to fornicate with her while her husband is absent.

"You are not answering my question," Mireille murmured.

He put down his cup, leaned toward her and tried to find the right words. "I'll tell you my truth, then you can tell me yours. You must know that I've wanted you ever since you arrived in Toulon, three years ago."

She looked out the window, suddenly interested in the passing traffic.

"Why do you think I've turned down your invitations to dinner?" Bastide continued. "Being with you and Jacques is like inviting a child to a birthday party and telling him he can't touch the cake. I know it's not a very flattering comparison, but it's the first thing that came to my mind." He glanced around the bar. "Now it's your turn," he said, finishing his coffee.

She reached out and put her hand on his forearm, increasing the pressure as she spoke. "I'm very lonely when Jacques is away. I think of you often. I . . . I imagine how it would be between us. Oh, the other officers try. They test me. But I can handle them." She looked at him, her eyes questioning and somber. "I don't know if I could handle you, Roger. Perhaps you're right. It is ridiculous. Two adults who want each other hesitating like schoolchildren." She made a despairing gesture.

Bastide took a deep breath. "Let's go to bed now," he suggested.

"What?" she asked, her eyes wide with surprise.

"You heard me."

"No," she told him, "not like that. After all these years, we're not going to end up in some flea-bitten *hôtel de passe* near the Opéra."

"We've got to do something," he said grimly, outwardly furious at her rejection but secretly pleased at her reaction.

"Jacques returns two weeks before Christmas," she told him. "That gives you some time to make a decision."

"Me?"

"Yes, you. My mind is made up."

She pulled on her coat and bent forward to kiss him. It was a lingering kiss. The tip of her tongue playing lightly over his lips sent a warm thrill through his body.

"I must go," she said. They stood up and embraced again, her thighs pressing against him.

"Roger," she told him, smoothing his tie, "I know you have another woman. But it doesn't matter to me. Your decision does. If it's no . . . I don't think we should see each other again."

She turned and walked quickly out of the café, leaving him frustrated and angry. His longtime yearning for Mireille Peraud had been brought to a head by a chance meeting that hadn't lasted more than a half hour.

The minstrel had taken up a position on the rue Aude. He'd been smoking Indian hemp, what his French friends called *kif.* It was a new experience. He'd sung two songs and they hadn't come out right. His words had gotten mixed up and he knew his beat had been off. He wasn't really there on the sidewalk. The part of him that counted was somewhere up among the chimney pots, floating quietly over the rooftops. He let himself slide down into a sitting position, his back against a stone wall, and contemplated the few franc pieces in his guitar case. It was a bad street for contributions, but he didn't mind. He'd come there because he knew the American woman would pass by on her way home. He'd thought of her a lot lately. She seemed different from the others, more mature, almost sedate, but he knew it was all a bluff and it irritated him. He would follow her and find out where she lived. He'd introduce himself, ask her to join him for a drink and find out the truth.

He peered up the street, hoping to catch sight of her, but it was too early. He closed his eyes for a moment, enjoying a feeling of light-headedness. His airborne self contemplated the streets from on high, observing the rush of two-legged ants far below. How stupid they looked! They were unimportant. They hardly deserved to hear him sing. With one nudge of his shoe, he could send a fall of sharp roof tiles and stones down on them, slicing them, crushing them, ending their useless lives.

The unexpected clink of a coin opened his eyes. A businessman had tossed it into the case as he passed. The minstrel watched the man as he disappeared into the crowd. Why had the fool done that? He hadn't even been playing. The minstrel stood up slowly and adjusted his guitar. If he wanted to invite the American woman for a drink, he would need more money. He was about to play when he saw the policeman watching him.

Claude Renucci had paused about thirty feet from the minstrel. He was standing with his arms folded, frowning with concentration. As the minstrel reached for his guitar case, Renucci moved forward. He was sure now that this was the same youth he'd seen earlier.

"*Vos papiers, s'il vous plaît,*" Renucci said, touching his cap with the grudging deference called for by regulations.

"I don't speak French very well," the minstrel responded, smiling.

"Your papers. Identity papers," Renucci demanded in hesitant English. Renucci examined the minstrel as he dug his passport out of an inside pocket. The young man was clean-shaven and comparatively well dressed for a street musician. He was a good-looking boy, but there was something strange about his smile. It seemed to be permanent and mechanical. Renucci took the proffered passport and leafed through it.

"You are American?"

"That's what it says."

Renucci compared the minstrel with the passport photo and checked the date of entry into France stamped on one of the pages.

"You have a *carte de séjour?*"

"I have a student card." The minstrel produced it, offering a silent thanks that he'd followed an American friend's advice to register at the university, even though he'd seldom attended a class. The short policeman seemed perturbed. He handed back the passport and student card as if he hated to give them up.

"Very well," he said, "now move along."

The minstrel, still smiling, cased his guitar and walked away slowly. Renucci watched him suspiciously. It didn't make sense. There was no doubt that this American matched the *portrait-robot.* But his papers were in order . . . he was definitely not a German. He swung around and headed back to the Cours Mirabeau. English, American, German or Scandinavian, they all looked alike. It was too bad. He wouldn't be rubbing the sous-brigadier's nose in anything for the foreseeable future.

CHAPTER VIII

The call from Nice caught Mattei as he was leaving the office. He sat on Bastide's desk while a detective described his conversation with Antoine Grimaud. The old man had been vague about his absent son, but he had remembered there was someone staying in his *cabanon* at Le Tholonet. He'd complained that his son's friends used the *cabanon* often without paying any rent.

"What did he say about the last visitor?" Mattei asked.

"He was particularly upset about him. Said he was an *Amerlo* and if anyone could afford to pay it was an American."

"Wrong. Our suspect is a German."

"Not according to Grimaud. He was certain his son had said his friend was American . . . a musician."

"How about the *portrait-robot?*"

"No use at all. The old man's never seen the guy. He's a mean old son of a bitch. Wanted us to throw the American out of the *cabanon.*"

Mattei was silent for a moment. First long hair, then short hair. First a German, now an American.

"*Allo, allo!* You still there?"

"Yes," Mattei responded. "Anything else?"

"No. That's it."

"Well, thanks. Anything new on that contractor's murder?"

"He was a *faiseur*, a heavy player in one of Grondona's casinos. He made the mistake of working with a croupier a few weeks ago and walked out with most of the bank. We haven't found the croupier yet, but he's probably horizontal too."

"Your Grondona's a real original."

"He's very touchy when it comes to his money."

"Thanks again."

Mattei put down the phone and tapped his thick fingers on the desk. He was still daydreaming when Bastide pushed open the door, a cigar clamped between his teeth.

"You're thinking, Babar!" Bastide remarked. "Are you sick?"

"Long hair, short hair," Mattei grumbled. "German . . . American."

"What the hell are you talking about."

"Nice called. They located old man Grimaud. He says our suspect is an American. His son told him before he left."

Bastide frowned, pushed some papers around on his desk, and looked at Mattei. "That's very vague."

"I know."

Bastide crushed his cigar into a chipped glass ash tray and walked to the window. "I suppose it still could be one of the Willington students."

"I doubt it," Mattei responded. "Lenoir has talked with them all. Most were at the party that night when the Feldman girl was killed. He's checked the others. Oh, Grimaud did say the *Amerlo* is a musician. Whatever he is, he's probably home by now in New York or Hamburg."

"Don't count on it. Remember, this character is on drugs. Magabian said he'd been high the day they fired him." Bastide came back to his desk and sat down.

"Long-haired, German or American, drug taker, a musician and living in Aix," he murmured, thinking out loud. "Where would you look for someone fitting that description?"

"On the Cours Mirabeau or around the market or the Palais de Justice."

"And what would our suspect be doing?"

"If he wasn't a concert pianist, he'd be playing for his supper on the street."

"Exactly. A street musician; they're contributing to tonal pollution all over Aix."

"But what if he is an American?"

Bastide shook another cigar from his leather case, incised the tip with his penknife and lit it. "An American," he mused, "and short-haired! Maybe we've got something."

"That *portrait-robot*, the short-haired version . . ."

"What about it?"

"There's one major thing wrong," Bastide said. "We labeled the suspect as a German. Every *flic* in the Bouches du Rhone has been looking for a *Fridolin* instead of an American. Just like they were looking for a long-haired hippie before we issued the second drawing."

Mattei sighed. "You're losing me."

"Never mind. I want a new edition of those sketches describing the suspect as either German or American. Put Lenoir on it. Call Guignon in Aix and pass the word. I don't want his people to waste time. Tell them the hunting season's been extended to Americans."

Mattei put on his cap and reached for his coat. "You going to lunch?" he asked.

"No. Send someone up from the canteen with a *sandwich de saucisson*, butter and mustard. And a small bottle of red. I'm eating here today."

Marcia Chappel had thought she'd never have been able to do it, but she had. It hadn't been a spur-of-the-moment decision. She'd thought of it that morning when she'd seen him singing near the Café les Deux Garçons. She'd been distracted all afternoon. Finally, when Dr. Gregg had left, she'd closed the office and hurried to the Cours Mirabeau to see if he was still there. He had been. She'd gone into the Deux Garçons for a cognac, still nervous and undecided. When she'd left the café, she'd walked straight to the singer with a determination that surprised her and asked him if he would join her for dinner.

He'd accepted with a puzzled smile. Now they were seated opposite each other in the Carillon Restaurant, a small bistro on the rue Portalis. She was excited, elated and nervous all at the same time. She'd been afraid of making a fool of herself, but he was acting as if her invitation had been the most natural thing in the world. She listened attentively while he told her of his adventures as a street singer. Once she'd made the decision, her hesitation and reserve seemed to have disappeared. Mark one for Dr. Sichburn, she thought, watching her new friend devour his *oeuf mayonnaise* and wipe the plate with a piece of bread.

The restaurant was warm and crowded, the wine was good and

Marcia Chappel was enjoying herself. He'd told her to call him
"Buddy." She was intrigued by his eyes. At first she'd found herself troubled at the intensity of his gaze, but she'd learned to accept
it and enjoy it. It was as if she were being caressed. A delicious
shiver passed through her body as he lifted his glass and toasted
her before attacking the grilled *entrecôte* and fluffy *pommes mousseline*
the waitress had put before him. She felt uninhibited and much,
much younger.

"The next time," he said, slicing his steak, "I'll invite you.
There's a good North African restaurant off the Cours Sextius. Do
you like *couscous?*"

"I really don't know North African food," she replied, finishing
her glass of wine.

"Tell me about you," he said. "I've been talking too much."

"Oh, I'm a working . . . girl. I'm with Willington University.
An administrative assistant."

The blue eyes held hers for a moment, then moved slowly downward, lingering momentarily on the buttoned jacket and the swell
of her breasts. She looked away quickly, nervously gesturing to the
waitress for another bottle of wine. She had a moment of doubt.
Had she gone too far? She'd never picked up a man before and . . .
he was so young. What must he be thinking? Was he laughing at
her?

"Willington . . . isn't that the group that had the student
murders?"

"Yes," she replied, not wanting to talk about it.

He seemed to sense her reluctance and changed the subject.
"Can I call you Marcia?"

"Certainly." She wondered if her newly purchased and carefully
applied mascara was still in place.

The minstrel watched her. She reminded him of his mother. The
same disgusting coquetry and self-consciousness; the same stupid
vulnerability. He was amused at the turn of events. He'd been
plotting to meet her and she'd approached him. He was sure about
her now. She was even worse than the others, hiding her lust under a façade of respectability. How many other young men had she
invited to dinner and to her bed? If he hadn't been so hungry he

would have lost his appetite. He hadn't really been listening to her as she babbled on.

"I'd seen you often on the street. I was impressed by your voice and I knew you must be an American," she continued. "It mustn't be easy for you . . . in Aix."

"Oh?"

"I mean—" She hesitated. "Well, not knowing where the next meal is coming from. You can't make too much . . ." Her voice trailed off.

"I don't," he said, filling his mouth with potatoes.

The cognac and the wine she'd already drunk produced a sudden, reckless honesty. "You know," she told him confidentially, "I've never invited a stranger to dinner in my life."

"You can't call me a stranger," he said. "We've seen each other often."

"You remember me?"

"Of course. The kind woman who always gives. I've watched you. I found you interesting. You're an attractive person."

She insisted he take dessert after their salad, and he polished off a large slice of *tarte aux pommes*.

"Would you like a *digestif*?" she asked.

"Only if you're having one."

She gestured toward the frosted windows. "We need something to keep out the cold." He let her choose. She ordered two green Chartreuses with their coffee. The strong liqueur burned her lips as she sipped it. He had delicate hands: long, tapered fingers and thin wrists. The hands of a musician. His suit was a little worn but clean. Where do we go from here? she asked herself. I've begun something, but I don't know how to finish it.

His mind was busy too. He yearned for a joint, and he wondered how soon he could get away from her. He'd had all he could stand for one night, but he knew he was going to see her again. The thought filled him with a welcome excitement. He would punish her. There was no doubt in his mind. But he would choose the proper time and place. This was the challenge that he enjoyed, watching them step into his web, squirming to be near him like bitches in heat. He'd missed that with the first one. He'd never

really known her. Punishment was only part of the pleasure. She
was talking again, but he barely listened.

"... ever leave Aix?"

"I'm sorry," he replied. "What was that?"

"Do you ever get out of Aix ... for a weekend?" She'd nervously taken another plunge. There was no going back now.

"Oh, I go to Marseille from time to time. Why do you ask?"

She rubbed at a wine stain on the paper tablecloth. "I sometimes
find it nice to relax, away from the town ..." she said, "...
away from my work. I've always liked the country."

"Yes, that must be nice."

She hesitated. He wasn't helping at all. She cleared her throat
and finished the last of her Chartreuse.

"Have you ever heard of the Château Bellevue?" she asked.

He shook his head, tilting his head, waiting for an explanation.

"It's not far from here. On the Durance River. It was an old
fortified farmhouse. The present owners have turned it into a
charming hotel with a one-star restaurant. I've been there twice.
It's peaceful and calm, with wonderful views from the rooms."

"Sounds nice."

"Yes." They sat in silence for several seconds until she raised her
head and met his eyes.

"Perhaps," she suggested, "if you're free, we could ... go there
together sometime."

His smile encouraged her and she returned it. "I'd like that," he
said, "but I really can't afford it. A *couscous* lunch is about all I can
offer ..."

"Oh no," she replied quickly. "It would be on me. No question
of your paying."

He laughed, shaking his head.

"What is it?" she asked, once again afraid he was laughing at her.

"Oh, it's the way things have happened. Every young man's
dream is to be offered a weekend with an attractive woman." He
pushed his coffee cup aside and leaned toward her, both elbows on
the table. "As they say in the films, we hardly know each other."

"I feel we can be ... friends," she said, surprised at her sudden
mastery of small talk.

Marcia Chappel nodded, her cheeks coloring. "Yes," she said softly, "somehow I do."

Claude Renucci was off duty, but he'd dropped by the *post de police* to pick up the pack of cigarettes he'd left in the pocket of his raincoat. He'd retrieved them, closed his locker and hurriedly walked through the hall to the door. It wasn't wise to hang around on your day off. Some overzealous superior might grab you for a special job or a fill-in. He glanced at the duty roster as he passed the bulletin board. A new notice had been posted. It displayed the same *portrait-robot* of the murder suspect, but something had changed. The poster was a little wider and more lettering had been added. He read aloud. "Of German or American nationality.

"Pardi!" Renucci exclaimed, glancing around the hall. There was no one to share his excitement. He hurried into a short corridor and knocked on a door.

"Come in," a gravel voice responded.

Renucci pushed open the door. The sous-brigadier was reading *Paris Match*, his uniform blouse unbuttoned, his chair pushed back, his feet braced against an open desk drawer.

"Aren't you off today?" the sous-brigadier asked.

"Yes, *Chef*, but I had to pick something up. Listen, about that *portrait-robot* . . ."

"Which one?"

"The one we talked about the other day. The German . . ."

"Et alors! What about it?"

"They've changed it. Now he could also be an American!"

The sous-brigadier heaved himself up out of his seat and buttoned his jacket. "Renucci, don't you have anything better to do than come in on your day off and spread confusion? I sometimes doubt your sanity."

"Look," Renucci said, leading the way, "I'll show you."

The sous-brigadier peered at the poster, frowning. "I haven't seen that one yet. They must have posted it when I was busy. So . . . he might be an *Amerloque?* So what?"

"I told you before. I stopped him, on the Cours. But I was looking for a German."

The sous-brigadier rubbed the gray stubble on his chin and readjusted his necktie. "I'd better tell Guignon about this," he sighed. "I don't suppose it means much. You stay here. In fact, you might as well put your uniform on. We're going to need you."

"*Merde!*" Renucci cursed as the sous-brigadier went in search of Inspecteur Guignon.

Hank Castel had been studying all morning. He'd decided to use Napoleon's return from Elba as a subject for a short paper he was writing. He'd never been particularly interested in Bonaparte, but an old manuscript he'd found in the university library had fascinated him. Its stained pages had been penned in sepia ink by an officer of the Old Guard, one of the faithful who had been with the Emperor on his march north at the beginning of the Hundred Days. The author had been surprisingly candid in his descriptions of the hazards and triumphs of Napoleon's great gamble. For the first time, Castel had been able to see "the Little Corporal" as a human being. He finished the last of his notes, returned the manuscript to the somber librarian and left the old building. Why was it all French librarians regarded their customers as potential thieves? Many of them seemed to think of their volumes as personal property, safe only when closed and secure on the shelves behind locked wire grilles.

He buttoned his jacket against the sharp cold and stepped out onto the street. A chestnut vendor's cart was on the corner. The wind fanned the red coals under the iron brazier, and the hot nuts steamed and popped, filling the air with their aroma. He rounded a corner and began to walk toward the Hôtel de Ville, wondering what Mr. Feldman had been doing since they'd last met. He stopped at a kiosk, dug deep in his pocket and bought a copy of *The International Herald Tribune*. He turned to the advertising pages to check the latest on cheap air fares. He was thinking ahead to his eventual return to the United States. With the dollar still high, it might pay to buy his ticket early. The ads for escort services far outnumbered any useful information on reduced fares. As he folded the paper and prepared to move on, he saw Marcia Chappel. She was talking to a young man with a guitar case under his arm. Castel was surprised. It was the first time he'd ever seen her with a man. They were obviously saying good-bye. The young man bent down to kiss her on both cheeks. Feeling like a spy, Castel decided to move on. He was horrified when he saw her coming in his direction, but he needn't have worried. She strode past without noticing him, a secret smile lighting her face. He'd never seen her look so young. Castel chuckled.

"Miss Chappel," he murmured to himself, "you're up to no good."

Roger Bastide was daydreaming in his own kitchen. It was just as well he'd planned a simple dinner. He was so preoccupied, he'd forgotten to pour himself the ritual glass of pastis. His trouble was women: Janine and her talk about their future; Mireille and the deadline she'd given him to make a decision. He stood for a moment, his hands on his hips, staring at the array of plump frog legs on his cutting board. He would prepare them in the Provençal manner, rolled in a light coating of flour and sautéed in hot oil until browned with a chopped garlic clove and a sprinkling of fresh parsley. That would be done just before serving. He sighed, slicing a lemon into quarters, and tried to decide what to serve with the frog legs. He chose to take the easy way out with *tomates farcies*. He selected three large red tomatoes from a basket on the sink, sliced them in half, seeded them, gouged out the pulp and dropped them into a small mixing bowl. He chopped a large onion, a clove of garlic and some parsley, adding them to the pulp. He walked to the frigidaire, opened it and stared at the interior, trying to remember what he was looking for. He finally reached for a leftover piece of ham, chopped it and added it to the mix with the yolk from an egg that he broke professionally, separating the white in half of the shell. He took a handful of bread crumbs from a glass jar, tossed them into the bowl, added ground pepper and salt and stirred the mixture with a wooden spoon.

"If it's no," Mireille had said, "I don't think we should see each other again." What did she expect him to do? Come rushing to Toulon, sweep into her villa under the watchful eyes of the neighbors and throw her onto the bed—Jacques's bed?

He worked slowly, filling each tomato with the mixture. When he'd finished, he covered them with a coating of bread crumbs, added a dash of olive oil and arranged them on a baking pan. They wouldn't take long to grill. He wiped his hands on a towel and walked to the window. Only then did he realize he didn't have a glass in his hand. He went into the living room, where he found himself staring into space once again. Janine would be there within the hour and he was busy worrying about Mireille! He reached for the pastis bottle but changed his mind. He could stand something stronger. He poured a generous jolt of Scots whisky into a short glass and walked back into the kitchen for a touch of water.

Normally, he felt a certain thrill in anticipation of Janine's arrival. A sort of erotic signal alerting him to what was to come. At the moment, he felt nothing.

"*Bon sang!*" he said aloud. "Between them, they're emasculating me!"

The telephone made him jump. It was Mattei. He seemed out of breath, his voice hard.

"*Pagaille!*" he told Bastide. "A mess! I've just been at Willington. That damn fool Feldman's in trouble. He attacked Dr. Gregg. He'd obviously been drinking. Luckily, I was there checking a file on the Bates girl. I was able to stop it. Feldman might have killed Gregg."

"Where's Feldman now?" Bastide asked.

"At the hospital. I had to tap him a bit."

"A bit?"

"He's still out."

Bastide raised his eyes to the ceiling. "How hard did you 'tap' him?"

"Well . . . he was going for a lamp. I caught him in the gut and brought him down with a chop. Nothing serious."

"For God's sake, try to keep the press out of it."

"I will."

"How's Gregg?"

"Swollen eye, a few bruises. No problem."

"Don't say, 'No problem'! I've got a problem. I've got to tell Aynard about it. That's a problem!" Bastide glanced at his watch. It was almost 7 P.M. He was sure Aynard was at home. He always left the office early on Friday night. Then he realized that he was being unnecessarily harsh with Mattei. After all, it wasn't his fault. If he hadn't been there, it would have been much worse.

"Babar," he said, "I'm glad you were there to handle things."

He heard Mattei chuckle. "He's a strong one, that Feldman. If he
hit me with that lamp, I'd have been under a doctor's care. One
good thing . . . Gregg isn't bringing charges. Well, I suppose
you'll want to contact Aynard. I'll stay in Aix until Feldman comes
around."

"Good. Call me, I'll be here."

"What's tonight's menu?"

"Grenouilles à la Provençale et tomates farcies."

Mattei bellowed with laughter.

"What's so funny?"

"Just before Feldman reached for the lamp," Mattei explained,
still laughing, "he called me a 'goddamned frog.' "

Bastide telephoned Commissaire Aynard at his home. Fortu-
nately he was on his way to a dinner at the Chambre de Commerce
and didn't have much time to talk. He did deliver a short lecture on
the dangers of police brutality, inferring that Mattei was prone to
use force when persuasion would have done the job. By the time he
hung up, Bastide was certain his call had awakened Aynard's stomach ulcer and the rich four-course meal awaiting him would put
him out of action for the weekend.

Marcia Chappel had been in the outer office with Mattei Friday
afternoon when Mr. Feldman had come by to see Dr. Gregg. It had
all happened quickly. They'd heard shouting, a curse and then a
crash. When Mattei rushed to open the door, she'd been right behind him. They'd found Gregg on the floor in a mass of scattered
file folders. Feldman had swung around, shouted something at
Mattei and tried to hit him with the desk lamp. She'd never seen
anyone subdued so quickly and professionally. The Frenchman
had stepped forward and in two quick movements Feldman was
face down and unconscious on the floor. At that moment, she'd
given up any thought of spending the weekend at the Château
Bellevue. Later, after Feldman had been carried off and Gregg's
bruises treated, Gregg had insisted she leave as planned. It had
been most considerate of Gregg after the shock of the assault. He'd
even offered her his car, a Volvo sedan, so she wouldn't have to pay
a high rental fee.

Now she was behind the wheel driving north from Aix toward

the Durance River. Saturday had dawned crisp and clear. The fields glistened with frost under a low sun. Wisps of steam hung over the streams and escaped from hidden hollows as the sun's rays filtered through the bare trees. Buddy had been waiting for her at the top of the Cours Mirabeau. He'd thrown his guitar case and a carrying bag into the back seat and climbed in beside her. She was pleased with the way he'd dressed. Casual slacks, a mustard-colored wool shirt, a tan foulard and a well-worn corduroy sport jacket. The shirt and foulard had been her gift to him when he'd admitted his best shirt was badly worn. She only hoped he was pleased with her appearance.

It had been a little difficult to break the conversational ice until they'd stopped for coffee and a croissant near Peyrolles. Things were easier after that. She was wearing large, baggy tweed slacks and a matching sweater she'd found in one of the chic shops on the rue Aude. She knew it was too young for her, but she'd seen the ensemble in the European *Vogue* and loved it. After all, this was a special weekend.

He sat quietly, watching the countryside and glancing occasionally in her direction. She drove well and seemed to be in a good mood. He thought her new clothes looked ridiculous. He'd noticed she'd used more makeup than usual. He wondered how it would all begin. She'd be more subtle than the blonde at Tholonet. This one, he told himself, wants to be loved . . . not just serviced. Then again, nothing might happen. A simple, platonic weekend in the country with good food and wine and no overpowering need to punish. It might be a tantalizing way of postponing his own pleasure.

"There it is," she said, pointing to their right, "the Durance."

He peered at the shallow water rushing past the stony banks and the leafless stands of thin trees. He was unimpressed.

"It looks cold," he commented.

"It is. But the *château* is warm and cozy."

He frowned, thinking of something she had told him earlier in the café. "So your boss was attacked?" he asked.

"Yes, by the father of one of the murdered students."

"But why?"

"The poor man is frustrated," she replied. "He's here to help the police, but there isn't much he can do, except . . . drink."

"And the police are getting nowhere?"

"I don't think so."

"How stupid!" he said vehemently. "They must be morons. No other profession would get away with it!"

The bitterness in his voice surprised her. She looked at him, frowning. "Goodness, I didn't know you felt so strongly about the murders. We've never really discussed them."

"I don't want to discuss the murders," he said, recovering from his outburst. "I just think the police are worthless."

"Well," she said soothingly, "let's forget the whole thing. We'll be at the *château* soon, in time for a terrific lunch."

The Château de Bellevue was on a hill about a quarter of a mile from the highway. It's thick stone walls looked down on a wide curve of the Durance. A jagged escarpment of rock protected the château from the mistral winds. The wide, raised terrace was used as an outdoor eating area in the summer and was now empty. All activities had moved into the vaulted halls and rooms of the château. Heavy, dark Provençal furniture lined the reception area. The walls were brightened by antique trays and kitchen utensils of polished brass and copper. A fire of heavy logs cracked and hissed in the wide hearth of the sitting room. A tantalizing aroma of good cooking seeped from the brass-trimmed door of the kitchen.

Marcia Chappel needed all her courage to ask for their room. The desk clerk's lack of interest in their marital status and his professional attempt to make them at home reassured her. They were led to the room she'd requested. It had a view covering more of the river. The mountains of the Lubéron hung over the late-morning mist like faint blue brushstrokes in a Japanese watercolor.

He noted there were twin beds in the room.

"Which is mine?" he asked.

"Take your pick."

He chose the one next to the window and pushed his overnight bag under the bed.

"Aren't you going to unpack?" she asked.

"Oh no, not now." He walked to a window. "This is great," he told her. "Just like you said. It's beautiful."

She smiled. There were times when he sounded like a little boy. It was endearing.

He took a deep, hot bath while she unpacked. He'd opened the window slightly to help dissipate the smoke from his joint of Indian hemp. The cold air formed a layer of steam that swirled over his head as he lay back in the porcelain tub and stared at the white plaster ceiling. For a few seconds he had a frightening memory gap. What was he doing? Where was he? These sudden vacuums of reason had troubled him lately, but they didn't last long. He pulled himself into a sitting position and reached for a towel. It would soon be time to act for his supper. He rose, dripping, from the tub and began to dry himself, examining his body in the wall mirror. He smiled at his own image and winked. It wasn't hard to understand why the women liked him.

Once he'd dressed and combed his hair, he searched through his carrying bag for a breath spray. He dug deep and recoiled suddenly, withdrawing his hand. Blood oozed from a small, neat hole on his right palm. He tore a piece of toilet tissue from the roll and stuck it on the tiny wound. Then he reached into the bag to cover the point of the ice pick with one of the hotel's bath towels.

Bastide was furious. Inspector Guignon had finally called to tell him that Renucci had seen the suspect. Obviously Guignon had kept the information to himself while his own men had tried to find the street singer. Now, over twenty-four hours later, he was admitting defeat.

"You're trying to tell me," Bastide shouted, "that you couldn't reach me?"

"Not exactly," Guignon hedged. "It's just that I thought a simple student pickup . . ."

"You're talking about a murderer!"

"You were so busy I decided—"

"Decided? It isn't your place to decide on a homicide case! Have you lost your mind? If you can't come up with a better explanation I'll have your ass on this one, and I'll see that it's sliced and diced!"

"I understand." Guignon said quietly.

"Good," Bastide said. "Now, if we're to pick up your pieces,

we'll need help. I'll want to talk to Renucci myself. You weren't
able to find a trace of the suspect?"

"It seems some of his countrymen know him. His name is Warren. He was last seen on Thursday. Renucci said he had a student
card. He's registered at the university, but he hasn't been attending classes."

"Do they know of him at the Willington group?"

"I . . . I don't know. We've been trying to find him on the
street. We did find his hotel. I've got it staked out—"

"Mon cher," Bastide said, addressing Guignon as if he were speaking to a new recruit, "I think it would be wise to get over to
Willington with copies of that police artwork and see if anyone,
professor, student or janitor has ever seen him. Ask Mademoiselle
Chappel to help you. Remember, the last time we were looking for
a German. Make it clear that this one is an American. It could
make the difference."

"I'm sorry about all this, Roger," Guignon murmured.

"So am I. If we don't collar this *Amerlo* quickly and he punctures
another young lady . . . both of us are in the shit!"

Bastide slammed the telephone down so hard that a chip of
plastic from the receiver flew across the office. He had planned on
a quiet Saturday to get his thoughts in order. Guignon's call had
killed that hope. Thank God he'd told Mattei to come in. He
glanced at his watch. Babar should arrive in another ten minutes.
He resisted the temptation to consider the case almost solved. All
they had was a suspect that *might* match a *portrait-robot*. And yet, he
probably had worked in Magabian's icehouse. He probably was the
rent-free tenant in the *cabanon* at Le Tholonet. If so, Bastide asked
himself, what was the motive? He pulled on his trench coat. Mo-
tives could wait. They would have to find the American first. He
took his detective Special from its belt holster and checked the
cylinder. The five .38-caliber messengers were in place. He made
sure the chamber under the hammer was empty as a safety precau-
tion and slipped the revolver back into his holster.

They began their luncheon with an apéritif of Kir Royale at a
table near the window. The dining room was a light salmon color,
the drapes were white and each table was decorated with a small

vase of red winter roses. The efficient, elderly waitress brought them a warm plate of hot *amuse-gueules:* crunchy almonds in crisp puff paste, small slices of pizza dough spread with chopped black olives and anchovy paste, cheese-filled pastry sticks. Marcia Chappel sensed the waitress was making a special effort. She guessed it was because she'd never seen her there before with a man. She sipped her Kir and watched her escort. He seemed strangely quiet. Perhaps he wasn't used to playing a gigolo. It must bother him.

"Cheer up," she said. "Why are you so quiet?"

"I guess it's all this luxury," he replied, surveying the dining room. "It's a long way from the Cours Mirabeau and a sandwich of *merguez frite.*"

When the maître d'hôtel arrived with the large menus, Marcia Chappel recommended the special gourmet lunch. It included fresh asparagus with hollandaise sauce, a casserole of sole and crawfish, a rack of lamb cooked with garlic and served with green beans, a garden-fresh salad of mixed lettuces, offerings from a cheese board rich in goat's cheeses and a selection of desserts heavy on ground almonds, black chocolate and cream.

"I'm game," the minstrel said, "but we'll need a long walk after eating."

She forced a smile. It was the first mention of what they'd be doing after lunch. It wasn't what she'd really had in mind. She crunched down on a cheese stick and shifted her eyes to the menu. She was irritated. She'd envisaged a romantic interlude following their luncheon. It was an old and honored French custom, a part of the culture that she'd never experienced. She wanted to make love to the man who was sitting across from her. To experience sex as she felt it should be, an amalgam of bodies, desires, heat, moisture, odors, maybe even pain. She glanced up at the minstrel and smiled. He noticed the softness in her eyes and read the unspoken message. It angered and revolted him.

"Shall we put ourselves in the hands of the *sommelier,* " she asked, "or would you like to order the wine?"

"Oh no," he replied, shaking his head. "Not me. I'm no wine expert."

Dr. Gregg wished he hadn't urged Marcia Chappel to take the weekend off. Hamish Forbes, the lawyer from Boston, had chosen to arrive in Aix without warning on Saturday morning. He'd found Gregg in his office, bruised, bandaged and busy with Inspecteur Guignon. Forbes had come to Aix via the Riviera, where he'd stayed with an old school chum for a few days. He was a rotund man who dressed like a character from an F. Scott Fitzgerald novel. Gregg's morale plummeted even further when he heard the lawyer's French. He obviously had supreme confidence in his language ability. Unfortunately his version of spoken French was an unintelligible mumble with Beacon Hill overtones that only confused the listener. Inspecteur Guignon was reduced to open-mouthed wonder as Forbes blithely assassinated the French language.

Gregg managed to move Guignon to Miss Chappel's outer office, where he could begin his interviews with the staff and students. His next task was to call in the *notaire* to take Hamish Forbes off his hands. Guignon had told Gregg that Inspecteurs Bastide and Mattei were on their way. He didn't want the lawyer around when they arrived. The minute Guignon left the room, Forbes shifted to English without a change of gears.

"So I thought . . . few days at Antibes would ah . . . with good friends. My aunt used to have a place near Aix. Assault case, I'd say. Must hurt? Too bad, but we'll handle it." He examined Gregg's bruises closely, lifting his glasses for a better look.

"I thought it would be best if you spend the day getting settled," Gregg said hopefully. "You can meet our *notaire*, Maître Salan. Perhaps you could get to know one another."

"I'd prefer to rest," Forbes said. "Had some late nights in Antibes."

Gregg was overjoyed. "Oh, by all means. After all, it is the weekend."

Forbes crooked a thumb toward the outer office. "Not very impressive," he whispered. "I've seen better police sergeants in Boston."

"We've got a room for you at the Hôtel Roy René. I think you'll like it."

"Well, if not, I can always find something else."

"I'll call a cab," Gregg offered.

"Don't bother. Got a car and driver." Forbes shook hands with Gregg. "It's good to meet you, Doctor. They think highly of you at Willington. I'll see you bright and early on Monday. Bye-bye."

Gregg sighed with relief when the door closed behind him. The man seemed controllable and far from a workaholic. Gregg touched his right cheek. It still throbbed. The doctor had told him he was very lucky to have come out of it without a broken bone. Thank God, Inspecteur Mattei had been there.

Gregg decided to go out for lunch. He'd let the police use his office as well for their interviews. He'd had a hard time rounding up both faculty and students. Many were away for the weekend, and everyone at Willington was fed up with being questioned about the murders. As he pulled on a tan cardigan and reached for his Irish fishing hat, he heard what sounded like an argument in the outer office. He thought he recognized Bastide's voice. Seconds later, his door burst open. Bastide entered in a cloud of cigar smoke. Gregg could see Mattei and Hank Castel behind him.

"What is it?" Gregg asked.

"Where is Mademoiselle Chappel?" Bastide asked, grim-faced.

"She has the weekend off."

"But where did she go?"

"She was planning to stay at the Château Bellevue . . . on the Durance."

Gregg resented Bastide's abrupt entry. "What's going on?" he demanded.

Bastide took the cigar out of his mouth and waved a *portrait-robot* with his other hand.

"This is what's wrong," he explained. "Monsieur Castel has identified this man. He saw him with Mademoiselle Chappel two days ago in Aix. He's our prime suspect."

"You mean . . . he might be with her?"

"He could be."

"It's highly unlikely," Gregg said, automatically erecting a barrier to more unpleasantness. "She isn't that kind of woman. I'm sure we'll find that—"

"We don't have time to speculate," Bastide cut him short. "Right now, it's a question of speed."

"Should I come with you?"

"No, it would be better if you remain here by your telephone. We'll keep you informed." Bastide turned and walked toward the door.

"Should I tell anyone?" Dr. Gregg called after him. "Our lawyer or . . . Mr. Feldman?"

"Tell no one," Bastide replied, "particularly not Monsieur Feldman."

CHAPTER IX

The police helicopter was late. Bastide paced back and forth, slamming his right fist into the palm of his left hand. They were waiting on a patch of open land not far from the Vazarely Museum. The sun had appeared, but a high wind was blowing over the hills surrounding Aix, bending the tall trees with its force. Mattei sat in the police sedan with the front doors open, eating a cheese sandwich and scanning the sky for the chopper. Guignon stood apart and alone, his hands deep in the pockets of his overcoat, watching the speeding weekend traffic on the nearby *autoroute*. They'd called the Château de Bellevue from Guignon's office. Yes, the American woman was a guest. Yes, she had a male escort. No, she could not come to the phone. The couple had just finished their lunch and gone for a walk.

"Here it comes," Mattei shouted, climbing out of the car, still chewing.

The chopper was approaching fast from the south, a speck in the sky that seemed to slide toward them sideways. The pilot swung wide, then dropped his craft abruptly, slowing his descent only when close to the ground. The landing skids crunched on the gravel and the rotor blades kicked up a zephyr of wind that flattened the surrounding grass. Mattei's cap flew off and he ran to retrieve it. Bastide hurried to the chopper and opened the cabin door. The helmeted pilot kept the rotors spinning. Bastide turned to Guignon, put his arm on his shoulder and drew him closer to shout in his ear above the din of the engine.

"You stay here," Bastide shouted, "in your office. We'll call."

Guignon nodded. Mattei had retrieved his cap and climbed in first. Bastide sat beside the pilot, secured the door, snapped his seat belt and put on a helmet equipped with a mouth mike. It was a relief to be cushioned from the noise.

"Château de Bellevue on the Durance?" the pilot asked over the intercom.

"Yes," Bastide replied, "and fast."

The pilot gave a thumbs-up signal, busied himself with the controls. The rotors spun faster, the engine produced a high-pitched whine. They lifted off the ground and rocked forward, climbing above the hedges, the trees and the *autoroute* before turning north over the tiled rooftops of Aix. The pilot handed Bastide a map covered with transparent plastic and poked at a red circle he'd drawn with a grease pencil around the location of the château.

"We can land in the parking lot of the château," the pilot told him, "or in a nearby field." He indicated a spot on the map about two hundred yards from the building.

"Not the parking lot," Bastide told him. "The field."

Below, they could see Route Nationale 96. Ahead was the aqueous ribbon of the Canal de Provence. Peyrolles would soon be in sight. Bastide was hunched forward in his seat as if he were willing the chopper to move faster. He knew he was dealing with the unpredictable. The man with Mademoiselle Chappel was probably deranged . . . *if* he was their man. But even with Castel's positive identification, there was no certainty that he was the murderer. He didn't want to alarm the suspect until he was well within their reach. Bastide looked more closely at the map.

"Can you see the field from the château?" he asked the pilot.

"I don't know. The owner only said they'd used it before for choppers."

"I'd like to land without being seen."

The pilot shrugged and looked doubtful. He reached over and took the map from Bastide. "There's a fairly high hill there," he explained, running his forefinger along some contour lines. I can try to come in from the east, keeping the hill between us and the château. It'll be risky in this wind and I don't know the state of the ground."

"We'll do it," Bastide said.

They'd followed the suggestion of the proprietor and taken the narrow path that led up into the rocky terrain behind the château. The minstrel had insisted on taking along a bottle of Hennessy from the bar to "toast the sunset." He'd packed it in his carrying bag. She'd thought it a good idea. Their lunch had been delightful. He'd come alive after several glasses of Chateauneuf du Pape. By the time they'd had their dessert and ordered a glass of cognac, she'd known the weekend would be a success. He couldn't seem to keep his eyes from her. Their feet had touched by chance under the table and she'd thought he'd pulled away, but he'd quickly made a joke about rushing the natural course of events. She'd understood what he meant. She was tipsy now and warm despite the wind. Why hadn't she thought of this before? she asked herself, regretting all the time that had been wasted.

"Hey!" he shouted, pausing to lean against an outcropping of ocher rock. "Let's not wait for sundown." He reached into his bag and produced the bottle, uncorking it and offering it to her as she climbed to his side. She giggled and took it, tilting it to drink. She coughed, laughing, and wiped a dribble of cognac from her chin. Then he drank three full swallows, closed his eyes and shook his head.

"That is good," he exclaimed. He pushed the bottle back into his bag and reached out to her. "Come on, they told us the real view is up on the top."

The cognac went through his system like molten metal. There was a ringing in his ears, but it was not unpleasant. When he'd gone up to get the carrying bag, he'd gulped some pills he'd bought in Marseille. He'd been saving them for a special occasion. The exertion of the climb and the accumulated alcohol had speeded their effect. He already felt like an eagle or a tiger or some mythical beast.

"Mythical beast!" he murmured smiling.

"What?" she asked, panting along beside him.

He ignored her question and gestured toward the rocks above them, urging her on. The starkness of the landscape fascinated him. It was raw and primitive. It reminded him of Mont Sainte Victoire. The trees near the summit were gray and twisted by the wind, deformed like the limbs of cripples. She had dropped behind now, head down, concentrating on the path. He looked over his shoulder at her and frowned. "Miserable slut," he murmured, reaching into his bag to feel the thin, round smoothness of the ice pick.

Guignon returned to his office. It was a beehive of activity. Plainclothes detectives were shouting over the telephones, the sous-brigadier was in radio contact with the gendarmerie at Manosque and all the available typewriters were in use. Guignon took off his hat and coat and sat at his desk. He picked up some telex messages and went through them quickly. The sous-brigadier finished his conversation and came over to make his report.

"All right for the roadblocks," he told Guignon. "They can cover the main roads on each side of the château. The Gendarmerie are pulling in some help from Cadarache."

"Did you tell them to stay well clear of the château itself?"

"As Inspecteur Bastide ordered," the sous-brigadier replied. "Our backup is on its way. Two cars. I sent Renucci along. They'll be in radio contact with the chopper once they get close. Oh, Monsieur Feldman is much better. The doctor suggests he be released from the hospital."

Guignon shook his head. "No," he said, "let him marinate for another twenty-four hours. It won't hurt him, and we don't want him on the loose with all this going on."

The phone on Guignon's desk added to the general din. Guignon nodded toward it, indicating the sous-brigadier should reply. When he did, he raised his eyebrows and made a grim face. "Yes, sir," he said deferentially. "Certainly. I'm not sure he's still here. Allow me a moment." The sous-brigadier put his large hand over the mouthpiece. "It's Commissaire Aynard," he hissed. "He wants Inspecteur Bastide or yourself."

Guignon put his forefinger to his lips and waved it back and forth with an emphatic negative motion.

"Monsieur le Commissaire," the sous-brigadier told Aynard, "I regret, but they are both out of the office. Yes, sir. Certainly. I will. I understand." When he'd replaced the receiver, the sous-brigadier made a fanning motion with his right hand.

"Well?" Guignon demanded.

"He is not happy. He wants Inspecteur Bastide to contact him immediately."

"It seems," Guignon commented, "that the Commissaire will just have to wait, won't he?"

"As you wish," the sous-brigadier said uneasily. "But he also asked for you."

"Oh no! I'm not going to take the venom meant for Bastide. Getting between those two is like walking into the middle of a Mafia feud. My dear colleague can cover his own ass."

The pilot brought the helicopter in close to the ground, trying to keep the hill as a blind. He swung and pivoted the chopper to avoid the trees and power lines in their path. At one point, he pushed the chopper up over a stand of cypress and Bastide caught a glimpse of the château's stone tower. The pilot slid his door open, examining the ground as they made their landing approach.

"It's too damp. Too much mud," he told Bastide. "If we land we'll sink in. You'll have to climb down." He pointed off to their right. "It's drier over there." He piloted them in that direction and descended toward the shiny, damp grass. When the skids were within five feet of the ground, the pilot nodded to Bastide. "That's it," he said.

Bastide unbuckled his seat belt and removed his helmet. "Where will you be?"

"There's an Esso station about three miles up the road from the château with enough space for me to put down. I'll stand by their phone. I'll keep in touch with your backup team from Aix by radio."

"Good." Bastide opened his door, grabbed the fuselage and swung out of the chopper, the wind whipping his trousers. He lowered himself till his feet touched the skids. For a few brief seconds he was back in Algeria, somewhere on a windswept plateau of the Aurès Mountains, going in for a helicopter assault with the paras. The image faded and he let himself drop the few feet to the ground. His shoes sunk into the mud and he cursed, staggering to keep his balance.

"Watch it," he shouted up to Mattei. "Let yourself down easy."

Mattei followed his advice, holding on to the skids till the last minute.

Once they were clear, the helicopter rose and flew off to the south. Bastide examined the terrain. There was a brush-covered draw on the far side of the hill. He tapped Mattei on the shoulder and indicated their route. They struck out, trying to avoid the patches of soft mud, their shoes squelching as they stepped from one patch of grass to another.

Bastide reflected on the irony of his careful planning. He'd wanted to be sure they would arrive unobtrusively. He'd instructed the pilot to avoid the parking lot. He hadn't wanted to draw anyone's attention. Now, after their trek through the muddy field, their shoes and trouser cuffs would be coated with drying mud. Hardly what you'd expect of two businessmen visiting the château at apéritif time.

They worked their way through the draw and stopped while still concealed by the bushes. There were eight cars in the parking lot. He identified the blue Volvo from the description Gregg had given him. No guests or staff were in sight. A dipping flight of starlings swept over the château and settled in the bare branches of an ancient oak. Bastide smoothed his mustache.

"Babar," he said, "we don't know if they're still on their walk or not. I'll go in by the main entrance. You get around in back in the event our *Amerlo* decides on a quick departure. I'll give you a few minutes." Bastide looked at the mud smears on Mattei's overcoat. "Try to look inconspicuous," he said. Mattei nodded and pushed his way through the bushes onto the driveway. Bastide smiled. No matter how hard Mattei tried he'd never look inconspicuous.

Bastide sensed the tension the moment he entered the hall and walked to the reception desk. The wife of the owner, a chubby blond woman with thick-lensed glasses, was biting her fingernails. She hadn't seen Bastide enter. She jumped involuntarily when he spoke.

"Madame," he introduced himself, "Inspecteur Bastide."

"Oh, *Bon Dieu!*" she whispered. "I'm so glad you're here."

"Where are they?" Bastide asked.

"They haven't returned. My husband has gone to the tower with his binoculars to see if he could spot them on the rock path."

"That is the path they took?"

"It's the one my husband recommended . . . before we knew. *Oh, là là,* Monsieur l'Inspecteur, I am frightened!"

"Calm yourself, madame. Things will be all right."

"But if he is a murderer?" she asked nervously, twisting her pearl necklace.

"We are not sure, madame," Bastide told her. He leaned over the counter. "What's that?" he asked.

"It's my husband's gun. He thought it wise to . . ."

Bastide moved behind the desk, picked up the double-barreled shotgun, broke it open, removed the two cartridges and slipped them into the pocket of his trench coat.

"You won't need it, I assure you. Where is the door to the rear of the château?"

"There," she said, "through the dining room."

He walked quickly through the reception hall, entered the empty dining room and opened the French doors onto the terrace. Mattei was waiting, half hidden by a hedge.

"Come on," Bastide said, motioning for Mattei to follow and running toward the rocks. "They're not here. Still on the walk."

"That's bad," Mattei volunteered.

"It could be," Bastide agreed.

The minstrel had reached the topmost rocks first. Marcia Chappel had stopped to rest about fifty yards below. He was panting but pleased with himself. He produced the bottle and drank deeply, savoring the strength of the cognac. He blinked in the face of the cold wind. The château looked like a toy castle from where he stood. He turned his head slowly to survey the countryside. Then he saw the helicopter. A glint of sunlight reflecting from its spinning rotors caught his eye and he watched it settle toward the ground. At first nothing particular registered in his mind. The distant craft resembled a cautious mosquito. He was about to shift his gaze elsewhere when the play of lights accented the colors. It was painted blue and white. Somewhere in the circuits of his drug-burdened brain there was a flash of enlightenment. He'd seen that type of chopper with those colors before . . . over the *autoroute* from Marseille to Aix. A police helicopter monitoring the rush-hour traffic!

He was still watching, fascinated, when the two men climbed down and the helicopter flew off. "Stupid bastards," he murmured to himself, watching the distant figures as they crossed the field and disappeared from sight.

"Hi!" she greeted him, still out of breath from her climb. "I thought I'd never make it." She put a hand on his shoulder to steady herself. He turned slowly. Her image was indistinct, out of focus.

"Someone," he said in a strangely quiet voice, "is always hunting the mythical beast."

"What *are* you talking about?"

"It's time for another drink," he replied.

"Good, I could use a pick-me-up."

She brushed some pebbles from a flat rock and sat down, breathing deeply. He wiped the mouth of the bottle with his sleeve and handed it to her.

"Do you consider yourself beautiful?" he asked, staring at her.

She laughed. "Of course not."

"Yes, you do."

"Don't be silly." She drank and returned the bottle.

"All women, even the most ugly, consider themselves beautiful." He drank again, looking over his shoulder to the field where the two small figures had disappeared from sight.

"Maybe you're right," Marcia Chappel agreed. "Maybe it's a form of self-protection." She thought he looked particularly attractive, like a Viking surveying his fjord. He had a wild quality that appealed to her.

"How many men have you screwed?"

The question hit her like a slap in the face. She turned pale and brought both hands up to her face as if protecting herself. Her mouth opened, but she said nothing. In the seconds of silence that followed, she desperately hoped she'd misunderstood him.

"Can't remember? Can't count that high?" he asked. His voice was flat and emotionless. Then he laughed. It was an unpleasant sound.

"Buddy," she said, rising from the rock to face him, "I don't understand. Is this some joke? It isn't funny—"

"How do you like it best?" He was sneering at her now. "What are you going to offer me tonight?"

"You've had too much to drink," she said with a quavering voice. "I think it's time we went back."

"You never answer questions," he continued. "That isn't nice. Only bitches don't answer questions. You must be a real bitch."

She turned to the path. "I'm going down," she said curtly.

His hand shot out and grasped her wrist. "No. You sit down on your rock and listen like a good girl." The pressure he exerted forced her to her knees.

"Stop it, please?" she asked. She was truly frightened now. Her eyes were wide, searching his face for a clue to his behavior. She found nothing but hate. She was suddenly filled with a desperate anger. "Damn it!" she shouted, trying to free herself. "Let me go."

Bastide thought he heard a shout. He stopped to listen, but the keening wind erased any further sound. He was a quarter of the way up the path. He'd sent Mattei to the other side of the rocks to cover any escape route. Bastide hurried now, climbing between the large rocks on each side of the path. He paused to remove his trench coat, rolled it into a bundle and wedged it in a crevasse. He moved his holstered .38 forward on his hip before resuming the climb. It was impossible to see the summit.

"No! No!"

This time there was no doubt. It was a woman's voice, etched in panic. Bastide broke into a headlong run. He vaulted the rough stone steps two at a time. He could hear his heart pounding, and his mouth was dry. Aynard was right. He should be in better shape.

She couldn't believe what was happening. If only it was a nightmare. She was flat on her stomach. He had one knee on her back, holding her down. She was struggling, but he seemed to have enormous strength. He'd torn her sweater and ripped off her bra. She'd tried to reason with him. He'd replied with a chain of obscenities whispered in her ear. She'd tried to shout for help, but he'd banged her head against the rock. She was sobbing now, slightly stunned.

"You slut," he growled, "you'll like punishment. You'll love it."

She tried to pray, but the words wouldn't come. She felt the shock of cold metal being pressed to her right ear. With sudden, horrifying clarity, she identified the object as an ice pick. Tensing every muscle, she shifted under his weight, kicked out and rolled to one side. He fell back onto his heels, steadying himself with his left hand. He lunged forward, the pick flashing through the air. She was backing away on her hands and knees but the point struck her, opening a gash on her chin. She felt she screamed at the sharp pain.

"I'm a mythical beast," the minstrel said in an eerie, conversational tone, gathering himself for another assault.

She jumped toward the path, stumbled and fell. She knew he was right behind her. He was still talking, but she couldn't hear what he was saying. She searched frantically for a stone to use as a weapon.

Bastide emerged from the path holding the .38 steady and aimed at the minstrel's chest. "Hold it there!" he ordered. Marcia Chappel retched onto the rocks as the two men faced each other.

"Drop it!" Bastide repeated, motioning with his revolver. "Now!"

The minstrel held the pick out toward Bastide. He seemed to be looking at it. Then he turned and ran. Bastide didn't fire. He wanted the American alive. He cursed and pounded after him.

"Go down!" he shouted over his shoulder to Marcia Chappel. "Quickly!"

The minstrel had disappeared behind some rocks. Bastide reached the edge of the escarpment. There was no path leading down the other side. It was a devil's maze of huge rocks and dead tree trunks. He heard the clatter of falling stones below and jumped down onto the slope. He slid on the surface of a flat stone, almost lost his balance, and grabbed for a gray tree branch to steady himself. It snapped off in his hand. He pitched forward, falling onto a scattering of jagged granite. His .38 flew from his grip, spun through the air and clattered among the rocks ten feet below. An explosion of pain seared through his ankle. He tried to get up, but there was nothing nearby to support him. He pulled up his pants leg to examine his ankle and tried to move it. The pain made him gasp. He had begun crawling toward a nearby rock when he heard someone approaching.

"Babar?" he shouted

"Lost your toy?" the minstrel asked. He was dull-eyed, his face slack. He held Bastide's .38 in his left hand and the ice pick in his right. "Don't move, policeman," he said coming closer.

Bastide watched him carefully. He knew he'd only have one chance. The important thing was to keep the American talking.

"You've made a mistake," Bastide said. "Let's discuss it."

The minstrel laughed and shook his head. "You're a loser," he said, "a nosy loser."

Bastide gauged the distance as the minstrel moved toward him, the ice pick extended. The numbing pain of his ankle would make it difficult. His timing would have to be perfect. The killer came closer. Bastide mustered all his strength and pushed his right leg forward, hooking the heel of his injured foot behind the American's leg. The pain of his effort made him shout in agony. He drove his left leg out, smashing it into his assailant's knee. The minstrel went down. Bastide pushed himself forward with both arms and clutched his opponent, his thumb and forefinger gripping the minstrel's throat. He grasped the revolver with his other hand, twisting it barrel up. One of the man's fingers snapped, trapped within the trigger guard. Bastide wrenched the revolver free. The minstrel wielded the ice pick. It slashed down, missing Bastide's ribs by inches, and buried itself in the ground.

"*Salaud!*" Bastide cursed, blinking through tears of pain and jamming the blunt nose of the .38 against the American's ear. "Enough, or your brains fly."

The minstrel went limp. Bastide released his grip on the man's throat and reached for the ice pick. He brought it forward till the blade rested just under the American's right eye.

For a second he had an urgent, almost overpowering desire to drive the ice pick into the man's skull. Then the minstrel began to laugh.

"*Ordure!*" Bastide said, crawling a few feet away, his .38 aimed and ready. "You don't deserve to live."

When Mattei found them, the American was rocking back and forth, holding his broken finger and singing softly to himself. Bastide, his revolver still leveled, had propped his ankle on a nearby rock and was smoking the last of his Cuban cigars.

Madame de Rozier left her desk and walked to the window. Heavy flakes of snow were falling onto the cobblestoned courtyard. The church bells were ringing, a fire crackled in the hearth and it was almost dark. She peered at her reflection in the window and adjusted her hair. A knock on the door caused her to turn. A mechanical smile creased her face. Her secretary ushered Dr. Gregg into her office.

"Do come in, my dear Dr. Gregg," she said, extending her thin arm to indicate he should sit down. "Would you like a glass of sherry?"

"No, thank you, madame." Gregg looked tired. He was still wearing a small bandage over his nose, a souvenir of Mr. Feldman's attack.

"What news of Mademoiselle Chappel?" Madame de Rozier asked.

"She is much better. She will be leaving for New England soon. The surgeon at L'Hôpital Nord doubts if she'll need plastic surgery on her face."

"It must have been a terrible experience."

"Without doubt."

"And that horrible Monsieur Feldman?"

"He's apologized to me," Gregg told her, "and returned to the United States."

"Well," Madame de Rozier said, sitting behind her desk. "I have just heard the good news about your grant. I am very pleased. You are indeed generous."

"Not me, madame," he corrected her, "it's Willington University."

"Yes, of course, but my dear friend, you *are* Willington in Aix."

Gregg acquiesced with a nod.

"Donating a memorial fund in memory of your, ah . . . departed students is certainly a noble gesture. It will allow our university's American-studies program to expand and improve. Something we have all hoped for."

Gregg smiled. The old bat was in prime form. A week before, she'd been trying to cut the Willington program completely. He knew she'd already begun negotiations with another American university group to take over the Willington buildings. But the

Boston lawyer had turned out to be a good judge of character.
Hamish Forbes had come back from his first meeting with Madame
de Rozier to suggest a gesture that might save the Willington program.

"That woman thrives on power," he'd told Gregg. "She's full of
her own imagined importance. Suppose we arrange to give her
another title?"

Gregg had been surprised at how fast Forbes worked once he
had a goal in mind. A flurry of transatlantic telephone calls and
some hurried meetings at Willington, and the lawyer had put a
package together. Funding for a new, expanded American-studies
program at Aix had been agreed upon, and Madame de Rozier
would be asked to be its coordinator. As Gregg listened to her
speak, he could see she had already taken on an air of added authority.

"Of course," she continued, "I was right about all this unpleasant affair?"

"How is that?" he asked.

"I told you it was someone from outside, no one having anything
to do with the university."

"Unfortunately, the murderer *was* an American," Gregg reminded her.

"Not really," she said. "Basically he was a German. But that's all
the past now. Tell me, Dr. Gregg, when do you suppose we can
inaugurate our new project?"

"Sometime next spring, perhaps in May."

"Really?" She pursed her lips in disagreement. "I would have
thought March would be better."

"I suppose that would be possible," he replied. "After all, you
are the coordinator."

"Yes," she said, "that is true, isn't it?"

Janine moved busily around Bastide's kitchen while he sat impatiently near the chopping block, nursing a pastis. He held a cane
between his legs and his ankle was encased in a short cast. He was
watching her every move and making suggestions.

"Put some chopped parsley on those potatoes," he said, "and the
sauce vinaigrette probably needs more mustard."

"Yes, sir!" she replied, giving a mock salute. *"Dieu merci!* I bought all this in the *charcuterie.* If I were trying to cook anything you'd be impossible!" In addition to the bowl of potato salad, she'd arranged a platter of cold meats and a plate of cheeses. There were slices of rare roast beef, mortadella, *saucisson sec,* Corsican *coppa* and thick chunks of *cervelas.* The cheese plate held a runny slice of Brie, a small round of Banon and a creamy Tomme de Savoie in its black rind. She took one platter out to the dining table. He reached out for her as she passed, but she avoided him, laughing.

"No time for that in this kitchen," she said. "Eating is a serious business."

"You should have opened the wine earlier," he shouted after her.

She came back and leaned against the kitchen door. "I'm going to be very happy when you can walk properly. For the moment, you're insufferable. How much longer are you going to be hobbling around with a cane?"

He finished his pastis. "Tired of nursing me?" he asked.

"Théo Gautier is in bed with the flu. When I leave him after fixing his broth and toast, I rush over here to see that you're not starving to death. It's as if I'm nursing two old men!"

"Don't exaggerate," he said. "I can move around. I can also get from here to the bed quickly, as you well know. The doctor told me I could be back in the office within three days. He only recommended I don't chase murderers on foot for a few weeks."

Janine brought a round, heavy-crusted loaf of *pain de campagne* to the chopping board and began slicing it.

"It'll do you good to get back to work," she told him. "You'll go mad sitting around here all day."

"On the contrary. I've read two books."

"A book on Northern Italian cuisine and the new Gault Millau Guide. I don't call that reading!"

"Do you suppose," he countered, ignoring her comment, "being this is a cold dinner, that we might eat sometime before midnight?"

"Go sit down. I'll bring everything in."

He hobbled to the table, sat down and filled their wine glasses with Brouilly. Butter, a pot of Dijon mustard and small bowls of black and green olives were already on the table. She brought in the salad, meats and cheeses and a *panier* of bread on a large serving tray. They touched glasses, sipped their wine and began to eat.

"Tell me," she asked, buttering her *pain de campagne*, "when will that awful killer be brought to trial?"

"I don't know. His defense will undoubtedly emphasize his mental condition. But he won't be going anywhere. Asylum or prison, he'll be locked up."

"I know it's terrible," she said seriously, "but I almost wish someone had . . . had eliminated him."

Bastide was remembering those few crucial seconds among the rocks when the telephone trilled from the bedroom.

"I'll get it," Janine said.

He continued eating, one ear cocked to pick up an indication to the caller's identity. Janine returned.

"It's Babar."

Bastide sighed, picked up his cane and limped to the phone.

"Roger?" Babar asked, "is it you?"

"No, it's François Mitterrand and you've just taken me away from a state dinner."

"Listen, Roger, normally I wouldn't bother you . . . The Antigang squad have just passed me some information. They've grabbed some of Grondona's people, *les Niçois*, bringing weapons into Marseille."

"Good for them. But I can't say it's earthshaking or unexpected."

"Normally I'd agree, but their *camionette* was stuffed with enough hardware to start a minor war. It included two cases of new Heckler and Koch submachine guns."

"*Bonne mère!*" Bastide murmured quietly. The H and K weapons were the favorites of terrorists. They were small, simple and easy to conceal. Their high rate of fire and spray effect ensured the death of any human target; it would also guarantee severe damage to much of the surrounding environment.

"Does Antigang expect trouble soon?" Bastide asked.

"Not till after Christmas. Then they've promised us a lot of business."

"I'd like to see their report on the seizure and a list of what they've got. Can you bring it to me tomorrow?"

"If I can squeeze it out of them. I'll call you before I come over. *Ciao.*"

"*Allez, bonsoir.*"

Bastide shuffled back to the table and dropped into his chair, frowning.

"Problems?" Janine asked.

"Yes," Bastide replied, staring down at his plate. "It looks like we'll be busy soon."

Janine shrugged and continued to eat. Although the prospect of a gang war in Marseille was disturbing news, Bastide's mind was elsewhere. Mattei's mention of Christmas had reminded him of something important. He'd missed Mireille's deadline by forty-eight hours. Her husband would have returned by now.

"*Alors!*" Janine waved her hand in front of his eyes. "Wake up!"

He raised his head and smiled. He suddenly felt relieved. Even if he'd wanted to take up Mireille's challenge, he couldn't very well have gone to Toulon with a cast on his ankle. Every naval wife in town would have noticed him and he'd never have been able to outrun an irate husband.

He put three slices of *coppa* on his bread and took a large bite. When he finished chewing, he lifted his glass.

"To my own personal *chef au froid,*" he toasted. "A fine meal."

"Ha!" Janine responded, "Straight from the *charcuterie* to the table. When are you going to let me prepare a real dinner from start to finish?"

Bastide assumed a mock-serious manner.

"Ma chèrie," he told her, "in the art of the table, as in love, nothing should be rushed."